OTHER DREAMS

- By -

Nicholas Ifkovits

To Sammy & Emma
Thanks!
Nicholas Ifkovits
4-16-98

Counter-Force Press

Mesa, Colorado

Counter-Force Press
POB 138
Mesa, CO 81643

Library of Congress Catalog Card Number: 96-96159

OTHER DREAMS

ISBN: 0-9651700-0-4

Manufactured in the United States of America.
10 9 8 7 6 5 4 3 2 1

Cover art by Dorsey Coe & Lee Bowerman.

Dedicated to all who have suffered the punishment
and pain of the falsely accused.

And a special word for the ladies of the Mesa County Library
Reference Center, who were so very helpful, and exhibited a
nearly amazing ability for tracking down the most obscure
information or tiniest fact.   Thank you for your generous
assistance.

Last, but certainly not least, I'd like to thank Jeff Inks of the
Promised Land for his 11th hour save when we encountered
technical difficulties just as this novel was about to go to press.
Thanks, Jeff. See you at the Chameleon Club.

OTHER DREAMS

*How is the faithful city become an harlot! It was
full of judgment; righteousness lodged in it; but
now murderers.*

- Isaiah 1:21

ONE

THE EGGMAN

The heat of mid-August had no mercy on the little town of
Harlot. It was hot and dry and the farmers of Northern Illinois
were pleased. The season had been perfect. The spring rains had
come right on time, just after planting, and the blessing had
continued with perfectly timed intermittence throughout the
summer. Now the corn was tall and healthy and emerald-green,
the long, slender leaves of the sturdy stalks rustling gently in the
breeze.

For the farmers this was the good time. The plowing,
planting, and cultivating were done, the fields well-dusted and
safe, and life was slow and easy waiting for the corn to dry in the
sun. If the weather kept up harvest would come early this year -
and a fortune in propane gas for the crop-driers would be saved.

In the meantime there were long mornings in Rachel's cafe
on the corner of Main and Mulberry streets. Sipping coffee with
friends. Discussing grain prices. The crop-perfect weather

and if it would hold. The new line of pickup trucks from Ford or Chevy and which was best. Maybe this afternoon get a 12-pack of beer, a fishing pole, and go down to Schlockrod's pond and cast for a few Bass or Bluegill. Time enough to grease the tractor and fix that lever on the combine tomorrow.

On the steps of O'Brien's Grocery and Meat Market, two doors down from Rachel's Cafe and directly across the street from Dirk's Hardware Store, Randy "Taterhead" Ellis stopped to listen. He liked the familiar, early morning sound of the birds chattering in the trees. Late summer was winding down. Soon it would be fall with its explosion of red, flaming-yellow and golden-brown. Hazy, musky days followed by crisp, clear autumn nights when the stars would shine like diamonds. Thanksgiving. Snow to shovel. Money. It was going to be a good year, too. Taterhead could just tell.

Randy Ellis' nickname, "Taterhead," was actually a derivative of "Mr. Potato Head," a moniker assigned him long ago by the other first-graders in his class because he so closely resembled the toy character. And he *did*. It was the shape of his head. Kind of round at the top, then going in at the sides right at eye level, then going out again, his two round cheeks the lower bumps of the "potato". And his nose. It was big and humped and rounded with a large nostril on either side just like the toy character's, and the whites of his eyes were large with tiny pupils, his mouth narrow with big red lips. Of course by Junior High the nickname had been shortened to "Taterhead," which, occasionally, was further reduced by the locals to simply "Tater."

But time had been kind to Randy "Taterhead" Ellis in other ways besides shortening his nickname. By the time he matured and filled out, his appearance became less drastic, his features softening to the point that most people entirely forgot *why* he was called Taterhead. One kid even thought it was because Taterhead Ellis simply ate lots and lots of potatoes. By 21 years of age, though, he wasn't a half bad looking young man.

Taterhead carefully shifted the egg cartons under his right arm and continued up the steps. The chalky white paint of the wood frame door was peeling, the bare wood beneath gray and weathered. A little bell attached near the top tinkled merrily, the four window panes rattling in their frames and the bottom scuffing against warped floorboards as he shoved the door open and went inside.

From the back of the store, out of sight behind the white enameled glass meat counter, a woman sang out, "I'll be right with you!"

Stopping just inside the door, Taterhead called, "It's only me, Mrs. O'Brien."

A round, rosy face cheerfully popped up. "Tater! I could set my watch by you!" she grinned. "Just a minute." She disappeared again.

Taterhead turned to the single check-out counter along the wall and carefully set his load of eight egg cartons on the soft, slate-gray surface worn smooth and slightly concave by innumerable, heavily-laden brown paper bags. Sniffling, he wiped his nose with a sleeve and reached into a small, pink plastic bucket full of Bazooka bubble gum near the cash register, removed a single piece and began unwrapping it. At 5'6" he was short and slightly built, but lean and strong from years of hard work. He had inherited his blue eyes from his father and his blond hair from his mother.

He popped the piece of gum into his mouth, looked at the joke, and then turned to the fortune at the bottom which read; *unexpected detour lies ahead.* Wondering just what sort of unexpected detour was in store for him (for he took the Bazooka bubble gum fortunes very seriously), he pocketed it for future reference. Then, whenever this bubble gum prophesy occurred, he'd have the proof that the predictions *did* work.

Just the other day he'd been arguing the point with his best friend, Gaitlin Tyler, who had ridiculed him at the very suggestion that there could be any significance in the silly fortunes printed on the bubble gum inserts. Still, Taterhead was convinced that there was some mysterious connection between him and them - a sort of cosmic guidance system that somehow reached him through the brightly colored wrappers.

The wait turned out to be brief. Taterhead was just weighing whether or not to spend another hard earned nickel on another piece of gum for later when Mrs. O'Brien came zipping up the aisle smoothing her white, beef-stained apron.

Taking her place behind the counter, she impatiently brushed aside a wisp of bright, auburn hair that had somehow escaped the tight pull of the single, girlish braid that fell between her shoulders, punched a key on the cash register and watched as the drawer popped open with a ringing clatter. "Let's see, eight cartons at .75 cents apiece, that's uhmmm. . . six dollars."

She snapped the bills out and laid them side by side on the counter. "See?" She smiled brightly and counted aloud, laying a forefinger on each dollar as if dealing with a three-year-old. "One, two, three, four, five, six!"

Taterhead had completed the counting even as she had been taking the cash from the drawer. Now, staring at the bills on the counter, his expression changed from a blank stare to a frown to one of passive acceptance as he struggled to quell the frustration of always being presumed stupid. Taterhead gathered up the money.

Assuming he'd been concentrating on the mathematical calculations of six dollars, Mrs. O'Brien laughed lightly, saying, "Oh, Taterhead! You don't really think I'd cheat you, do you?"

Folding the bills into his hip pocket, Taterhead unthinkingly commented, "Anyone's capable of an honest mistake, Mrs. O'Brien."

"Of course." Her smile was thin. She was always quite nice to this slow-witted zero that nobody much liked. And he always came back uppity. Not an ounce of gratitude for her genuine kindness. She had shelves to stock. "Will that be all?"

At her clipped tone he stopped and looked up. Not wishing to make yet another enemy, he replied humbly, "Yes ma'am, unless I can do anything else for you."

She opened her mouth to speak but caught herself, changed tack to a cheerful disposition and said, "There is one more thing you could do for me, Tater. Bullets is supposed to mow the grass this morning. Will you stop by the house, see that he gets up and remind him about the grass for me? He's been sleeping later and later and I'm afraid he's getting into a bad habit."

Taterhead nodded. "Sure, Mrs. O'Brien. I'll be going by your house around 9:00 o'clock."

"Thanks, Tater. See you tomorrow morning, then."

"Bye, Mrs. O'Brien." He turned to leave, remembered the bubble gum and turned back exclaiming, "Oh, I almost forgot!"

She had already started from the counter to continue the stocking chores and wheeled around, asking impatiently, "What now?"

Gesturing at his mouth and the bubble gum he was noisily chewing, he dug out a nickel and handed it to her. "Gum."

"Oh, thank you, Tater."

For the second time he nodded goodbye and turned to leave, the bottom of the shaky door scuffing against warped floorboards, the windows rattling, and the little bell tinkling as he went out.

OTHER DREAMS

TWO

ERICA STRUTS HER STUFF

13-year-old Erica Erickson, all finely chiseled features, full lips, pale hazel eyes, and long, straight, light-brown hair, was well developed beyond her tender years, with rounded hips and firm, up-thrust breasts stretching the fabric of her black and yellow Batman T-shirt so tightly the perfectly round nipples were clearly defined. A child with a woman's body, she was just learning to bleed even as her two constant companions, 13-year-old Kevin Crisper and 12-year-old Johnny Bulger, were learning that their wieners were good for something besides peeing with.

Had Erica foreseen the morning's events she probably would have worn a bra. But that would have spared her a certain amount of perceived humiliation and consequently, the full sympathy of the crowd, who would have been less entertained and less in need of assuaging their own guilty consciences.

But none of these things troubled the minds of the three plotting adolescents as they stood across the street from O'Brien's Grocery and Meat Market. Tater's old red Ford was right out in the open in the middle of town and someone might see them. Had they just nonchalantly walked up to the truck and taken three cartons, no one would have batted an eye even if they *had* noticed, presuming that the kids were supposed to be taking the eggs. And even Taterhead wouldn't have missed them until near the end of his route when he came up short. By then the kids would have been long gone and he himself simply mystified. But, neophyte thieves that they were, they hesitated and thus were surprised by Taterhead as they stood at the side of his old Ford helping themselves to his eggs. He knew all three.

Shouting "Hey!" as he leapt from the stairs, it flashed through his mind like a red neon sign; *the unexpected detour!* Startled, the three kids bolted, scattering up the street in three different directions, each with a carton of eggs under one arm. Confused, running after first one, then the other, Taterhead quickly realized he was only going to catch one and focused on the Bulger boy.

But the kid turned out to be faster than Tater thought. With pounding heart and sneakers slapping the pavement, he managed to catch up to him at the end of the block. Rounding the corner, he grabbed him by the collar, but their feet became entangled and both tumbled to the warm, tacky asphalt, the egg carton crunching between them and vomiting raw egg into both their faces.

Taterhead came out on top, sitting astride Johnny's chest. Both were scuffed and bleeding, but that didn't stop Taterhead. Grabbing the front of Johnny's shirt, he shook him furiously, shouting, "Those are *my* eggs! Why ya takin' *my* eggs!?"

Johnny Bulger was squirming and crying, "Lemme go! Lemme go ya weirdo!"

Still furiously shaking the boy and demanding payment, an egg suddenly smacked Tater in the forehead, drooling like snot down his face as he looked up in startled surprise to see a grinning Erica standing several feet off and winding up to throw another. The second egg splattered against his chest. Then another smacked the back of his head, raising goose bumps as it dribbled down his back. Whirling around to see Kevin Crisper standing some ways off behind him, soon both kids were pelting him with eggs just as fast as they could throw them.

With Taterhead distracted by the massive egg assault, Johnny managed to squirm free - almost. As Taterhead came back around, Johnny punched him square in the nose. Taterhead tumbled backwards, tears springing to his eyes as Johnny leapt to his feet shouting jubilantly, "Look! He's cryin'! I beat up Taterhead Ellis!" And with that he ran laughing up the street loudly crowing this achievement to all. Dropping their empty cartons, Johnny's companions ran after him with hoots and hollers at this tremendous triumph over Taterhead Ellis.

Dazed from the sucker punch but angry as hell, Taterhead sprang to his feet. Slipping and sliding in the puddle of raw egg, one sneaker screeched against the pavement as he gained traction and took off after them.

Flush with confidence, Erica was loping along at the tail of the herd and Taterhead easily caught up. Furious, he grabbed her by the hair and spun her around.

Shocked and frightened, she frantically flailed and kicked, accidentally hooking one long, carefully nurtured fingernail in a tiny hole in the front of her T-shirt, scoring one breast a bloody scratch as the shirt ripped halfway down the front before breaking the nail. But she hardly noticed, gleefully cracking him in the shins and smacking him in the face, all the while shrieking like a stuck pig, "Get offa me! Leave me alone, ya weirdo! HELP!!!"

With Kevin and Johnny excitedly leaping and dancing around them shouting taunts, Taterhead lunged at the girl, engulfed her in a bear hug and held her fast to control her furiously flailing limbs. "Stop! Stop, now!" he cried in a frightened voice. When at last she ceased struggling, Taterhead, thinking she had given in, let her go.

Bellowing, "How *dare* you touch me!" Erica whirled around and kicked him in the balls, scoring a direct hit. Gagging,

Taterhead doubled over and dropped to his knees as Rachel's Cafe emptied into the street.

Oblivious to the onlookers quickly gathering on the sidewalk, the three adolescents encircled him like a pack of snarling wolves. With Johnny driving in, delivering a punch to the side of the head, and leaping clear, Kevin did the same from the opposite side, while Erica viciously and repeatedly kicked him in the back.

Mesmerized, the crowd of onlookers shifted and rolled with every movement of the fracas, staring goggle-eyed - not at the boy on the ground, but at Erica's perfect adolescent tits, which had swung free of the tattered black and yellow T-shirt, one streaked a bloody scratch clear to the pink, upturned nipple.

So engrossed in the attack were the assailants, and the onlookers in Erica's breasts, that nobody noticed the Jefferson County squad car come roaring up the street. Not until it screeched to a stop, hot tires swirling blue smoke and the stench of burnt rubber. And then big old Hal Rankin leapt out shouting, "Here! Stop now! Stop that!" and rushed forward waving his hands like an umpire signaling a slider safe.

Johnny Bulger and Kevin Crisper immediately backed off, but not Erica. She continued flailing and kicking at Taterhead, who was lying curled up on his side, alternating between shielding his nuts and covering his head, his forearms going up and down like some kind of weird, mechanical wind-up doll.

Anxious, confused, hesitant to physically touch a nearly naked teenaged girl in front of a crowd in the middle of Main Street, at last officer Rankin took a deep breath, threw his arms around her from behind, pulled the apparently hysterical girl off and dragged her back several feet.

But he was only holding her lightly. Carefully. Like a China Doll. As the dumbfounded cop and a wide-eyed community looked on, Erica suddenly twisted free and thrust her breasts out, the nipples growing erect as she strutted like a proud rooster beneath the noses of the crowd. "Look!" She cried, "look what Taterhead Ellis did to me!"

But she wasn't a rooster. She was a hen. You could tell by the tits.

OTHER DREAMS

THREE

ADDING INSULT TO INJURY

Buster and Jane Ellis were not a happy couple. The Ellis farm, which Buster had inherited from his father, who had inherited it from Buster's grandfather, who had inherited it from *his* father, had quietly and insidiously slipped through his hands. Year after year, parcel by parcel, Buster had sold it off to pay his debts. Debts he was never quite able to get on top of. And then one day he woke up very old and very tired, the dreams of success swirling away like a puff of smoke.

The farm was gone. Except for 10 acres and the huge, 150-year-old tumbled down red brick two-story farm house, its ornate, hand-carved wood trim cracked and gray, the last curling chip of chalky white paint having blown away years ago.

And all his friends were gone. Dead. Or prosperous and far removed from his social station. Failure. It ate away at his insides like acid, corroding his heart and rotting his soul, leaving him a bitter old man with watery, bloodshot eyes, wispy white hair and wrinkled gray skin.

Thus would he spend the last of his days, wandering about the huge, dark house that smelled of mildew and cat piss and rotting wood. Clutching his beer, bumping into furniture and mumbling to himself in a constant and bitter refrain.

His frail, bony wife was as gray and beaten as he was. She fed the cats and washed the sheets. (He peed in them every night.) She cooked the meals (and mostly ate them by herself, too), washed their clothes, and sat in the living room in her favorite chair in the bluish glow of the softly burbling TV, a single bulb from the floor lamp beside her casting a feeble yellowish light on the open page of her bible. Reading. Gently rocking. Waiting to die. . . .

Fate had been cruel to Buster and Jane Ellis. Their first born ate a mortar shell in 'Nam. Their second ate a tree out on the highway at high speed. A total waste of good beer, Buster would cackle drunkenly on a certain Saturday each November. A Saturday that always seemed to be windy and cold, damp and gray.

And then there was Randy. "Taterhead," as everyone called him. Of his three sons, the only one that survived turned out to be, well, different. Buster Ellis didn't like him. But Buster didn't know that. Could never admit that. It just was. And so they were. Mumbling and stumbling. Reading and rocking - when a knock came at the door.

Gripping the doorknob tightly, Buster Ellis swayed back and forth, caught his balance, took a swig of beer, swayed some more and pulled the creaking old door open. Blinking against the sudden flood of brilliant morning light, Buster squinted up at the big, uniformed officer who stood hat in hand, an old-timer with a big belly and wisps of gray at the temples. A man Buster once knew but now didn't recognize.

"Buster?" Hal Rankin inquired, his voice rising.

"Yeah?" Buster replied sardonically, "what'a *you* want?"

It wasn't common practice for the county to send out an officer to inform someone about an arrest, but Hal Rankin had known Buster and Jane Ellis socially many years before and felt a need to personally explain what had happened to their son. Now the big man cocked his head slightly, inquiring curiously, "Don't you recognize me?"

Buster looked the man up and down. "Well. . . yeah. . . I think maybe I seen ya somewheres before."

Poor old Buster. "I'm Hal Rankin of the Jefferson County Sheriff's Department," he began, deciding a businesslike tone might be best.

Buster stared at him for a moment, gently swaying as if moved by the breeze, then squinted an eye and said, "So? What'a you want with me?"

"It's about your son, Tater. . . er, Randy."

Buster's gaze wandered, the hand gripping the doorknob trembling so hard the knob rattled. Momentarily turning his attention to the beer can in his other hand, he took a healthy swig, exhaled a great blast of raunchy beer breath and looked up at the man again. "So?"

Thin and frail, her face like a wrinkled old bag, Jane Ellis shuffled to her husband's shoulder from the depths of the dark, rank-smelling house. "Buster's not feeling well," she said, the corners of her mouth quivering with a weak smile, the effort of which seemed to make her head dip briefly.

Her husband half turned towards her and stood aside indignantly as if to say, *who invited you into the conversation?* After a moment he turned back to the officer, smiled brightly and inexplicably raised his can in a jovial gesture. "Join me in a beer, officer, uh, what did you say your name was?"

Looking uncomfortable, Hal Rankin shifted his weight and cleared his throat before uneasily declining. "No. Thank you, Mr. Ellis." He took a deep breath before continuing. "I'm here about your son, Randy. We're holding him at the county lockup."

"Ohhh. . . . " Jane Ellis' face went slack, her eyes glazing over as one trembling hand reached for the support of the door frame.

A tender touch the old woman hadn't felt in years, but now her husband absently handed the officer his beer can and moved to her side. A protective arm about the shoulders, he drew her into the house, imploring of the officer as he went, "Please, come in," and gently guided his wife to the scarred old rocker where her bible lay.

Rankin tentatively stepped just inside the door and stopped. It was unbearably hot in the dark, closed up room, the air like thick, rancid syrup.

With his wife seated, Buster straightened up and impatiently beckoned the man into the living room, saying with a gesture towards Jane, "Please, my wife."

At this point wishing he had telephoned instead, Rankin, only two years from retirement, came into the living room, the floor beneath his big shiny black shoes creaking and groaning with every step. He handed Buster his beer and sat down at the opposite end of the couch. Holding up his hands, he looked at both of them and admitted, "I don't know where to begin."

"What did Randy do?" Mrs. Ellis pointedly asked.

"He. . . . " Rankin faltered. "He's charged with criminal sexual abuse of a minor."

The old woman jerked perceptibly, the bible slipping from her fingers and falling to the floor with a thump.

"He raped a child?" Buster's voice quavered on a high note.

"Oh, no, no, Mr. Ellis. He. . . he only, uh, fondled her upper body area," the officer stammered, then regained his composure and decided to get this over with. "According to the juvenile's statement, he tried to lure her and two friends into a sexual liaison by offering them free eggs. Well, the kids took the eggs, but when they declined sexual favors he became violent and attacked the children."

"Oh no!"   Her eyes welling up with tears, Jane Ellis anxiously looked around the room, twisting this way and that as if the old rocker were holding her fast and she needed to escape.

"Now, now, Mrs. Ellis.   Calm down.   Randy denies everything," Rankin quickly explained.   "He claims he caught the kids stealing his eggs."

Buster was trembling so hard Rankin could feel it clear through the couch and the floor beneath his feet.   In a scratchy high voice edged with panic the dishevelled old man asked, "Well, did he *do* it?"

"I guess that's for a judge and jury to decide," the officer answered forthrightly.

Buster Ellis sighed with what Rankin could have sworn was relief - or maybe, rather, with a sense of, *well, it's all over now.*

"The charge is not as serious as it sounds," Rankin put in.

"Well if he did do this thing, whatever, sexually attacking a child," Buster's voice was strong now and tinged with indignation, "we want to see justice done, too.   We don't want our boy going around messin' with no kids like that.   No sir, we want to see him before the judge just as much as that little girl's folks do!"

"Well that's very noble," Rankin bobbed his head once.

"Yes," Jane Ellis put in, giving a defiant nod of her own tousled gray head.

"But you're going to need a lawyer."

"A lawyer!" Buster screeched, "a lawyer! Lawyers cost a lot of money! Do I look like I got a lot a money around here?"

Rankin lifted a shoulder and sadly shook his head.   "I don't know what to say, Buster."

"Can you bring Randy home for us, sir?" Mrs. Ellis innocently asked.

"I'm afraid not, ma'am. You see, he's been arrested. He's in the county jail. Bail's been set at $5,000 dollars."

"$5,000 dollars!" Buster cried, "I don't got $5,000 dollars!"

"No. You only *need* $500 dollars. Ten percent to get him out. You don't have to come up with the other $4,500 unless he runs."

But by now Buster was shaking his head disdainfully. "Get outta here," he waved the man off. "I don't have that kind'a money to throw away 'cause Randy's feelin' up some kid."

Nervously toying with his big brown Stetson, which he held by the brim between his fingers, all at once Rankin stood up and put it on. "I'm sure sorry about this, folks."

"$5,000 dollars," Buster mumbled, getting up and staggering in the general direction of the kitchen and his beer supply, "get outta here."

"I'm really sorry about this, ma'am," Rankin said, bowing slightly towards the old woman.

But she was staring across the room, face rigid, eyes unseeing.

There wasn't anything further to discuss. With the floor boards creaking and groaning beneath his big black shoes, officer Hal Rankin quietly left, closing the door behind him.

OTHER DREAMS

FOUR

THE LEGEND OF BULLETS O'BRIEN

Jim O'Brien would never retire. At 58 he felt like he was just hitting his stride. His large, comfortable, contemporary home, newly built only six years previously, sat on 15 acres where he raised a variety of fruit trees, including apple, peach, pear, plum and cherry, with which he supplied fresh fruit to his own store, O'Brien's Grocery and Meat Market in town. (100% profit on those items.)

He also had an additional 40 acres under cultivation, purchased from Buster Ellis the previous fall, and now raised his own produce as well. And the crop was good. So was life. While he tended the orchard, the crops, and maintained the equipment, his wife, Anna, ran the store.

Jim O'Brien blew the horn a second time and peered up at the huge, rustic stone and timber home he was so proud of. Women! Sometimes he felt he spent half his life just waiting for them to get ready. He glanced at his watch impatiently. He had to be back by 5:00 PM.

He was just about to lean on the horn again when the front door flew open and his daughter, 18-year-old Colleen, came bounding out, the bright auburn hair she had inherited from her mother flying as she ran lightly down the broad shallow steps of the terraced stone walk. Jumping into the pickup truck, she breathlessly exclaimed, "Okay daddy, I'm ready!"

"All right, sweetheart," he smiled at her. "You excited?"
"Yes! Oh yes, daddy, thank you!" she cried, leaning over with an embrace and a kiss.

"Okay, none a that mushy stuff!" he laughed, pulling out of the driveway, tires spitting gravel as he quickly accelerated.

"You drive so fast!" his daughter remarked.

"Everyone in our family drives fast, including *you,*" he grinned at her.

Although secretly disappointed in his son Kelsy, commonly known as "Bullets" for reasons Jim O'Brien thought rather dubious, he was enormously pleased with his daughter. A popular girl in high school and graduating near the top of her class, she was already registered at Northern Illinois University and would be leaving in a week.

And now father and daughter were off to Freeport to pick up the new (used) car he had arranged to buy for her. His treat as a reward for her excellent academic performance, and a belated graduation gift. She would have gotten it last spring but Jim O'Brien, a man who carefully managed his money and avoided bank loans whenever possible, hadn't had the cash on hand.

But it was just as well, he reasoned, because it had given them plenty of time to shop around, although he wasn't completely pleased with the car his daughter had chosen. He'd had his eye on a big Buick which he considered safer because of its size. But it was red and she wanted blue, and the Toyota *was* two years newer with 30 thousand fewer miles on the odometer. And for the same money. So the Toyota it was, even though it didn't have an air bag.

*   *   *

Kelsy "Bullets" O'Brien groaned and rolled over, burying his head beneath his pillow. In the brief moment he opened his eyes he could tell it was afternoon by the angle of the sunshine streaming through the window. Who the hell had opened his curtains like that? Probably his mother. She'd been nagging him recently about sleeping late. And not having a job other than the little chores and odd-jobs he picked up here and there around town.

Kelsy O'Brien earned a permanent place in local folklore and acquired the nickname "Bullets" four years previously when only 17 and a senior at Harlot, Illinois' tiny high school. That was the year when, while visiting his cousins in Chicago some 130 miles to the southeast, he surprised two burglars, or so legend had it, and took four .22 caliber bullets to the midsection at pointblank range. All four bullets had blown clear through without hitting any vital organs or even bones, which would have shattered the bullet (as well as the bone) and sent it ricochetting through his body, ripping up a lung or kidney, destroying his intestines, blowing out his heart, or at least destroying a few muscles and leaving him with a game arm. Instead he *still* drove off the burglars, or so legend had it, and although leaking a lot of blood, grabbed a pint of Jack from the kitchen, walked four blocks to the bus stop and took old number seven to the hospital.

Now, four years later, Kelsy "Bullets" O'Brien was still a local folk hero. Someone the youngsters (and even the oldsters) looked up to. Bullets the invincible. A legend in his own mind. The part local folklore left out was the truth. The lie about the burglars had been concocted by Kelsy himself when his aunt and cousins came home to find him lying on the kitchen floor full of little holes, bright red blood misted in four small circles across the cabinets and counter tops, puddles on the floor.

The ripoff Kelsy single-handedly engineered had backfired. Inexperienced with the big city and drug dealing, he thought he was going to take two small-time thugs to the cleaners for two ounces of sifted baking soda, flour and sugar. Being his first drug deal of any kind, it had never occurred to the lad that they'd snort a bit before parting with their $3,500. Too bad his mother hadn't allowed him to watch *Miami Vice* when he was growing up (too violent), then at least he might've had sense enough to put a little *real* cocaine in a separate Snow Seal for the inevitable taste-test.

Instead, after snorting Kelsy's concoction, the two petty thieves/cocaine addicts simply pushed their chairs back and stood up, one drawing a small, .22 caliber revolver from his jacket pocket and popping four rounds into the teenager. Gagging with heart-stopping fear, the boy dropped to the floor in a dead faint, which probably saved his life. Presuming him dead, the thugs left.

It wasn't that Kelsy "Bullets" O'Brien was a bad kid - he was a rat. A snake in the grass. The kind that would sell his own mother for the right price. And at 6'1" he was tall, dark and handsome, with long, wavy dark brown hair, an easy grin backed by two rows of straight white teeth, and deep brown eyes in a soft, rosy-cheeked face that tanned easily. Thus did 21-year-old "Bullets" O'Brien command attention wherever he went. Girls got shy or giggly around him. Boys got wary or subservient. With his elevation to folk hero status four years previously, the rat had been made king - of Harlot, Illinois. Everybody loved Bullets. Even his own mother.

One thing was sure, though. Getting shot was the best thing that ever happened to him. Since then life had been pretty easy. His grades even went up that year, although to his recollection he hadn't studied any harder.

And the funny way everyone looked at him his first day back in town after getting released from the hospital in Chicago. At first he didn't know what to make of it. But then, even the doctors and nurses had been amazed at his rapid recovery. Hell, he'd only spent three days in the hospital. *Three days!* After being shot *four times!* And then it dawned on him why they were looking at him funny. They thought he was, like, *invincible* or something. Like he was God's own son. Incredibly, he then went on to lead the high school basketball team to a series of roaring victories that snagged the championship of their small rural conference that year.

Of course the rumors began to circulate from his first day in the hospital. Then, over the next three days as he lay recovering, friends and relatives started calling, and Kelsy, without even realizing it at first, began embellishing the tale - and a legend was born. The legend of Bullets O'Brien.

After a moment Bullets heaved a sigh and peeked out of his lair at the clock radio on his nightstand. 2:00 PM. Time to get up, shave, shower, dress, eat and head for town and the Gray Wolf Tap where everybody met afternoons after work.

By 4:00 PM, belly comfortably full, rosy and fresh scrubbed in clean denims with his favorite black, button-down shirt and a pair of new work boots he'd recently bought, Bullets stepped out onto the porch of the sumptuous luxury home his parents were so proud of and took a deep breath of sweet, late summer air.

And then he noticed the grass. It was long and getting longer. He was supposed to have cut it this morning. Oh well. Tomorrow. Reaching overhead with a knuckle-cracking stretch, Bullets released a big breath of air, started down the terraced stone walk and cut across the grass to his car.

He slipped behind the wheel, slammed the door and turned the key. Instantly the 390 CI V-8 came to life with a throaty rumble from the dual exhaust. After pausing a moment to let the oil circulate, Bullets put the car in gear, rolled out of the driveway, and gunned it down the blacktop for town.

He had received the hot-looking metallic blue '72 Ford Torino as a gift from his grandfather three months ago for his 21st birthday when grandpa had decided it was time to get one of the newfangled high-mileage cars. Quite literally, he *had* only driven it to church on Sundays and once a week to town for groceries.

When Bullets drove out to Iowa with his dad to pick it up there were only 62,000 miles on the odometer. Luckily for

Bullets, when grandpa had gone in to trade, a cocky young salesman *62,000 miles!* presumed the old timer had no idea the value of the vintage early-70's hot wheels his rather plain Ford coupe had evolved into over the last two decades or so. A real choice piece of collector's rolling stock, the salesman thought he was going to soak the old man on the trade-in. That's when grandpa decided to give it to his grandson for his birthday.

Now, with a set of mag wheels and four Goodyear Eagles to match, headers, chrome side pipes and a new, gleaming metallic-blue paint job, Kelsy "Bullets" O'Brien had the hottest car from Jefferson County to the Mississippi river.

OTHER DREAMS

FIVE

LIFE AT THE TAP

A quarter mile down the road from the Ellis place, George and Marybell Tyler had a modest two bedroom, aluminum-sided white frame home on the Birchwood Blacktop. They had moved in when Gaitlin was four, taking over the operation of Harlot's only gas station. Gaitlin and Taterhead had been friends ever since.

While George did most of the wrenching himself at the little service station, high school boys that came and went through the years pumped the gas and fixed the tires for minimum wage and the chance to work on their own cars after hours. Thus was George Tyler able to eke out a living.

A fair, honest, hardworking man with a loving wife, he had managed to instill these virtues in his son, Gaitlin, who hadn't been without some form of summer or after school employment since the seventh grade.

In the four years since graduating from high school, Gaitlin Tyler had worked as a laborer for a utilities construction contractor. It was brutally hard work, and at 5'9" the quiet, soft-spoken 22-year-old was compact and well built, every rippling muscle sharply defined. But his conservative dress of loose-fitting cotton print shirts hid the taut body beneath. And narrow brown eyes like straight lines behind black plastic-framed eyeglasses thick as coke bottle bottoms, a wedge nose, thin lips and mousey brown hair cut in a rather practical style that was no style at all, made him look like a skinny, nerdish bookworm type.

Although it was his custom to stop at the Gray Wolf Tap for a beer or two after work, he pretty much kept his opinions to himself, and no one had ever seen Gaitlin Tyler drunk. It wasn't that he held his liquor so well, he just wasn't a big drinker.

When Gaitlin rolled into town in his shiny new black Dodge Shadow with the driver's side air bag, a car he'd purchased only three weeks previously, he was surprised at the large number of pickups and cars angled up to the curb out front of the Gray Wolf Tap. Mondays were usually pretty slow, as everyone was still recovering from the heavy partying and ensuing hangovers of the weekend.

Like many small town gin mills in the Midwest, the Gray Wolf Tap was long, narrow, dimly-lit, and smelled of stale cigarette smoke, beer, some kind of strong chemical cleaning agent, and human urine.

As one entered from the south off Main Street, the serving bar and red upholstered stools were on the left, running almost the entire length of the west wall. A long row of booths were on the right along the east wall. Where the booths ended the take-out beer coolers began, the four heavy glass doors flush with the wall. Beyond the serving bar and coolers the room opened up, with a pool table in the center and a jukebox, bowling machine, and two pinball machines along the west wall. The opposite wall had two wooden doors heavily painted chocolate-brown, the first labeled *Pointers,* the second, *Setters.*

When Gaitlin came in with a strobe-like blast of bright sunlight, the spring-loaded door slamming shut behind him, everyone in the crowded bar looked up, the buzz of heated conversation curiously fading as he stood there blinking behind his thick, coke-bottle eyeglasses. His eyes adjusting to the dimness, Gaitlin sauntered over to the bar. Something odd was going on.

Lowell Bordewith, proprietor and bartender of the moment, had greasy black hair with a perpetual cowlick in back and a red nose swollen from years of heavy drinking. With a nod he said, "Afternoon, Gaitlin" and took a quick slug of his drink.

"Lowell," Gaitlin returned the nod, tossed some bills down and added, "Bud."

"Right," Lowell smiled friendly, popped open a bottle, set it on the bar, took the bills and returned with the change as the buzz of conversation resumed. "Heard what Taterhead did?" he asked, leaning against the edge of the bar with both hands.

"No."

But before Lowell could get into an enraptured explanation of the events of the morning, Bullets, occupying a center booth with three of his cronies, called out, "Hey, Gaitlin!" and beckoned with a wave of his arm.

Momentarily distracted by Bullet's call, Gaitlin turned back to Lowell and said, "Looks like I'll be hearing about it soon enough," gave the man a nod, grabbed his beer and crossed to the booth where Bullets sat next to Henry "The Weasel" Hillard, a rat-faced carrot-topped little sneak with pale, freckled skin, green eyes and two prominent front teeth. Across from them sat Nathaniel "Nervous Nate" Naumann, tall, lanky, and perpetually worried, and Bartholomew "Fat Bart" Binks, a dumpy, greasy kid with bad skin, bad teeth, and bad breath.

"Well, move over and let the kid sit down," Bullets said with a gesture that motivated Nervous Nate and Fat Bart to slide closer to the wall.

"Thanks," Gaitlin said, slipping into the booth beside Nervous Nate.

Everyone took a swig of beer before Bullets intoned, "I take it you didn't hear what your best friend did this morning."

"Nope," Gaitlin said, shoving his glasses back on his nose, "just got off work."

With a sigh and a half-smile Bullets shook his head and looked up. "Taterhead tried raping Erica Erickson this morning."

"What!?" Gaitlin's mouth fell open as he looked around the table in shocked surprise.

"That's right," Weasel grinned, giving Bullets the elbow. "Tore the shirt off her back right in the middle of Main Street. Grabbed her tits and everything."

"He just went crazy," Nervous Nate put in. "Scratched one of her tits really bad, too."

"You should'a seen it," Fat Bart crowed, "I was there!"

"What!?" Gaitlin exclaimed again, utterly dumbfounded. "No way!"

"Yes way," Bullets grinned. "And everybody in town seen it too, including Hal Rankin."

"Who's Hal Rankin?" Gaitlin looked at him.

"You know, the old sheriff's deputy."

"Oh yeah, right." And all at once, *"He* was there, too?"

All four boys nodded with grimaces that were really smiles, Bullets adding, "Just as Erica and two of her little friends," he suddenly stopped with a big show of perplexity and turned to Nervous Nate, "who were they?"

"Johnny Bulger and Kevin Crisper."

"Yeah, Rankin showed up just as Johnny and Kevin were beating him off."

"And we're not talking about a hand-job!" Weasel grinned.

"Although that might'a been what Tater was looking for," Nervous Nate volunteered. "All three kids said he tried to lure them into his truck. Said he'd give 'em free eggs if they'd go out to Tess's Grove with him and take off their clothes."

"What!?" Gaitlin exclaimed for the third time. "It don't make sense!"

"Hey," Weasel shrugged, "he's a weirdo, what can I say?"

"They freakout once in awhile and do crazy things, ya know?" Nervous Nate added.

"Yeah, but not Tater!" Gaitlin said heatedly. "I've known him all my life. He wouldn't do something like that in a million years!"

"Yeah? Well tell that to my daughter."

Gaitlin suddenly felt a huge warm hand on his shoulder. It was Axl Erickson. He was standing just behind Gaitlin, and he was smoldering.

"Yeah, tell that to Erica," Weasel wisecracked.

Behind his thick, horn-rimmed eyeglasses, Gaitlin blinked, then twisted around to look up at Axl. "Hi, Mr. Erickson," he said nervously.

At 6'2", 357 pounds, Axl Erickson was a big man with a large round head and a marine crewcut. Plumber by day, beer drinker by night, his beer belly was even bigger than his mouth. He was known as something of a braggart and barroom brawler who never walked away from a fight - as long as the other guy was smaller. And he always wore a trademark 10-inch buck knife sheathed in hand-tooled leather to match his hand-tooled belt. A large rectangular silver buckle embossed with *Axl* completed the ensemble.

"Don't 'hi' me, pal," Axl snorted, offended. He was feeling the buzz of his 10th beer as well as the buzz of being the center of sympathetic attention since he'd come into the place at 3:30 that afternoon. Now he had a focal point for the self-righteous indignation that had served him so well all afternoon. "Everybody in town," he gestured with a wave of his hand at the roomful of people, "saw him do it. Are *you* gonna sit there and tell me he didn't?"

Gaitlin took a deep breath and slowly let it out, shrugged and said nervously, "I didn't mean anything except that it doesn't sound like something Tater would do. That's all I meant, Mr. Erickson."

Axl frowned darkly. "Well he did do it."

Gaitlin stared at him. "Well I wasn't there," he said after a moment, "so I wouldn't know."

"Yeah? Well *I* was there," Fat Bart huffed, "and he had Erica's shirt torn open right in the middle of Main Street. Only about a dozen people saw it!" he added sarcastically.

Gaitlin whirled on him. "You actually *saw* him grab her shirt and tear it open?"

Fat Bart dropped his eyes and shrugged a shoulder. "Well, no," he admitted, "it was already tore when I got there."

"And you, Weasel," Gaitlin cast his eye on him, "did you actually *see* Taterhead tear her shirt open?"

Weasel shook his head. "I wasn't even there."

With everyone in the joint suddenly listening to their conversation, Gaitlin quickly turned to the room at large and loudly asked, "Did *anyone* see Tater actually rip Erica's shirt?"

The room was dead silent.

"I saw him chasin' all three a them kids down the street," a voice from the back piped up. "Ran right past Rachel's place when I was havin' my mornin' coffee they did."

"Who's talking?" Gaitlin called out.

"It's me, Bud Winkle," a grizzled old man said as he left his stool and stepped out of the circle of attentive onlookers that had formed. He was janitor at Saint Christian's Church, a huge, barn-like white structure with a small clapboard grade school and minister's residence overlooking the town from the hill at the end of Main Street.

"And did you see *why* Tater was chasing the kids?" Gaitlin pointedly asked.

Bud Winkle thought for a moment, scratching his bristly chin with a thumb and forefinger, then shook his head. "Nope, can't say as I did. Just seen the three of 'em run past, one, two, three, with Tater chasin' 'cm. She still had her shirt on then," he hastened to add with a delighted chuckle.

Bristling at Bud Winkle's apparent pleasure in his daughter's public humiliation, Axl made a move towards the man before several hands reached out to restrain him, someone saying, "Easy Axl, Bud didn't mean nothin' by it."

"No, not at all," Bud Winkle quickly volunteered, dipping his head once and taking a small, nervous slug of beer.

Gaitlin turned back to Axl and raised his shoulders. "See, Mr. Erickson? No one really saw what happened or how her shirt got torn, that's all I meant before."

"Yeah?" Axl cocked his head, "so what're you sayin', my daughters a liar?"

"Oh no, of course not, Mr. Erickson."

"Well that's what it sounds like to me, 'cause *she* said he tore it and was tryin' to feel her up!"

With Axl glowering, Gaitlin suddenly decided it was time to change the subject. Seemingly on impulse he turned to the four boys in the booth with him, shoved his glasses back and asked, "Where is Taterhead, anyway?"

At that everyone chuckled, Axl saying with the disgust one reserves for the exceptionally dimwitted, "He's in jail."

With a brief glance Axl's way, Gaitlin inquired of the boys at the table, "In jail? *Still?* I thought it happened this morning?"

"It did." Bullets put in.

"W - Well. . . ." Gaitlin stammered, "didn't anyone bail him out?"

Bullets gave him a look like, *who'd want to bail him out?*

"Do his parents even know he's in jail?"

Several heads nodded.

"And even *they* wouldn't bail him out?" Gaitlin looked around the table.

"Hal Rankin said even his own parents think he done it," Axl said evenly, taking a swig of beer. "Looks like you're 'bout the only one in town has any doubts."

Meekly looking at the man, Gaitlin offered in a small voice, "Well maybe if we talked to Tater. . . ."

"Tater?" Axl sneered.

"Well he was there, too," Gaitlin retorted lamely. "I mean, has anyone even talked to Tater about what happened?"

Nobody said a word.

Setting his bottle on the table, Gaitlin got up and started past Axl for the door.

"Just where the hell are you going?" Axl stopped him with a huge hand to the chest.

Glancing down at the hand on his chest, Gaitlin had to tilt his head back to look up at the big man. "I - I'm going to talk to Taterhead," he hesitantly admitted.

"Yeah? And then what?" Bullets rose from the table and came around Gaitlin's other side.

Gaitlin looked at him. "I'm not sure yet," he answered, once again pushing his glasses back. He was beginning to sweat and they kept slipping down his nose.

Bullets took a threatening step closer. "Not sure?" he sneered. At 6'1" he was a good four inches taller than Gaitlin, but that was the absolute extent of any physical advantage he might enjoy. Bullets had never done a lick of hard physical labor in his entire life, and the only athletic activity had been high school basketball four years previously, the years since having been given to beer and pot and lounging in front of the TV. As a result he was soft. Soft in the arms, soft in the legs, soft in the middle and soft in the head. In any test of combat with Gaitlin he'd be hard-pressed to come out looking anything but silly.

But Gaitlin didn't know that, or rather, was intimidated by Bullets' size and the myth of the other boy's invincibility. After all, if .22 caliber bullets didn't faze him. . . . "I - I'm not sure what I'm going to do yet," Gaitlin stammered again.

"I wouldn't go bailin' him out," Axl warned darkly.

Caught between the two of them, Gaitlin looked from one to the other, then quickly shook his head. "I doubt I'll do that."

"Good, 'cause if you do I just might cut *it* off," Axl snarled, suddenly brandishing the gleaming 10-inch hunting knife. "That way there won't be no danger a him attackin' some kid again and rapin' 'em!"

At that the crowd broke into hoots and cheers and applause of encouragement, Bullets hissing in Gaitlin's face, "And I'll help him!"

Gaitlin worriedly stared at them for some moments, nodded okay and eased past them for the door.

"And ya better watch out what side you're takin'!" Bullets hollered after him as the door slammed shut, "'Cause that buck knife'll work on you, too!"

At that the drunken crowd once again hooted and laughed. Grinning triumphantly, Bullets turned and raised a victorious fist in the air before taking his seat.

As the spring-loaded door banged shut behind him Gaitlin heaved a sigh of relief. Deciding he'd better see what his dad had to say before heading down to the county lockup to talk to Taterhead, he stepped off the stoop and crossed the street to his father's gas station.

"Hi, Sammy," Gaitlin said as he strolled through the glass door propped open with a big yellow phone book.

Leaning back in the chair with his feet up on the desk reading a comic book, the sandy-haired youth glanced up. "Hey, Gaitlin." Then, "Did ya hear what happened to Tater?"

"Heard all about it," Gaitlin replied, sitting with one leg on the corner of the desk.

"Oh." The boy seemed disappointed that he wasn't going to get to tell the story again.

"Did you see what happened, Sammy?" Gaitlin asked, pulling his glasses off and rubbing at a sweaty itch on his forehead with the heel of one hand.

"Nahhh," he replied dejectedly. "I always miss the good stuff. I was an hour late this morning, otherwise I would'a seen it."

"See?" Gaitlin grinned, putting his glasses back on, "if you hadn't been late you would've seen the whole thing."

"I know, but if I'm never late again for the rest of my life nothin' like that'll ever happen again," the boy sighed. Looking up, he added plaintively, "Everyone got to see Erica's tits."

"So I've heard," he paused. "Say, is my dad around?"

"Yeah," the kid gestured with his head, "in the garage."

"Thanks," Gaitlin said, sliding off the corner of the desk and heading for the shop.

To the curiosity of many Harlot residents Gaitlin had never worked at his father's service station. It wasn't that they didn't get along or had problems working together, it was just that Gaitlin had no special interest in cars, wanted something more physically demanding, more money, and had no intention of taking over the family business when his father retired.

"Hi, dad," Gaitlin said as he sauntered into the garage.

Squatting by the front wheel of a Chevy and mounting a wheel cover, George Tyler spoke over his shoulder. "Hi, son. What's up?"

Gaitlin waited until his father pounded the cover on and stood up, then asked, "Did you see what happened this morning with Tater? Everyone's saying. . . ."

"I know what everyone's saying," his dad interjected. "Must have been a dozen people by with the news this morning, and no, I didn't see what happened."

"But. . . ."

"I was in the middle of a tune-up when all the commotion started. I glanced out the garage door once, but all I saw was a crowd of people down the block towards Rachel's Cafe. I guess it was pretty much all over by the time I looked. At least the fightin' was."

"So you didn't see *anything?*"

George Tyler shook his head. "Nothing."

"Hmmm," Gaitlin frowned for a thoughtful moment, then looked at his father. "Well, do you believe what they're all saying? That Tater tried luring those kids into Tess's Grove and tore Erica's shirt off and everything?"

Pulling a shop rag from his back pocket and wiping his hands, his father heaved a sigh and shook his head. At last he looked up. "Doesn't sound like the Taterhead I know."

"My feelings exactly," Gaitlin agreed, adding, "poor kid. I heard even his own parents think he's guilty."

"That so?" George Tyler looked at his son.

Gaitlin nodded.

"That's too bad. But I wonder if they have reason to? I mean, maybe Tater's been acting strange lately or something. Ya know, like, I don't think the kid's all there sometimes."

"He's a lot sharper than people give him credit for, dad," Gaitlin said earnestly. "He's got this reputation for being slow or something, but it just takes him a minute to get his words out, and people tend to write him off before he gets the chance."

"Well has he?" His father looked at him.

"Has he *what?*"

"Been acting strange lately? I mean, if anyone would know you would."

"No, he hasn't," Gaitlin answered rather defensively, "and I personally don't believe a word of anything I've heard so far about what happened this morning."

Moving to the big sink at the back wall, George turned on the water and pumped hand cleaner into one palm. "So what's your theory?" he asked, rubbing the cleaner between his hands.

Gaitlin shrugged. "At this point I don't know. I was planning on heading out to the county lockup and finding out, though. Straight from the horse's mouth if you know what I mean."

His father nodded and turned to rinsing his hands.

"My question is, if I hear what he has to say and think he's innocent, should I bail him out?"

His father shut off the water, snapped some paper towels from the dispenser and dried his hands. "I think that would be a noble gesture on your part. After all, you guys have been friends for a long time."

"Yeah, I know, but I just came over from the Gray Wolf and everyone there was, like, *threatening* me if I should bail Tater out. Especially Mr. Erickson and Bullets."

"Bullets?" His father asked in surprise. "What's he got to do with all this?"

Gaitlin shrugged. "Nothin'. Far as I know he wasn't even there this morning."

George Tyler shook his head in disgust. "He's just a meddler, stickin' his big nose into it. You know, I think he's gotten a big head ever since he was shot in Chicago. Course that's no surprise the way people carry on about it, but it don't make 'em God, far as I can see, it just makes 'em he got lucky is all."

"You're right about that," Gaitlin agreed. "Anyway, Mr. Erickson pulled out his big hunting knife and threatened. . . ." he faltered.

"Yes?"

"Threatened to castrate Tater if I bailed him out."

"Oh," his father scoffed, waving him off, "that's just drunk talk and his sudden popularity goin' to his head."

"I don't know," Gaitlin looked doubtful, "he sounded pretty serious to me."

His father shook his head. "No. You just do whatever *you* think is right and never mind about him. He's just a bully."

Gaitlin nodded. "Thanks, dad." He turned to leave but stopped, adding, "I'm heading to the lockup to talk to Taterhead then, so tell Ma I'll be late for dinner."

"Okay, son. Drive careful."

"I will. Thanks, dad. Bye." He gave a little salute like they always exchanged and left.

OTHER DREAMS

SIX

A FRIEND IN DEED

"I didn't do nothin'," Taterhead protested. "All I did was try to get the money out of 'em for stealin' my eggs!"

Gaitlin looked unsure. "Johnny Bulger, Kevin Crisper and Erica *all* said the same thing, that you tried luring them out to Tess's Grove, offering them free eggs for sex, and after you gave them the eggs and they wouldn't go with you, ya kind'a went nuts, chased them down and started ripping at Erica's shirt." He paused, looking at his friend through the bars. "Is that true?" he quietly asked.

Taterhead rolled his eyes in disgust. "Come on Gaitlin, you know me better than that! Course it ain't true!"

"Then why are those kids saying it, Tater?"

Taterhead stared at him, then shrugged. "I guess 'cause they want to get away with stealin' my eggs - and what they did to me." He sniffled and wiped an eye, adding, "Now they got it all turned around like *I* did somethin' wrong instead a it was *them* that did somethin' wrong!"

Gaitlin looked at his friend for a long, silent moment, then asked softly, "You *sure* you're telling me the truth, Tater?"

Randy "Taterhead" Ellis solemnly nodded.

"The *whole* truth?" Gaitlin pressed.

Again Taterhead nodded.

Letting out a long breath of air and gripping the bars, Gaitlin looked at his friend. "If I bail you out where will you go?"

"I don't know. Home, I guess."

"What about your parents?"

"What about them?"

"Well, the way I understand it," Gaitlin began cautiously, "they think you're guilty too. Will they let you back in the house if they think you tried raping Erica Erickson?"

"Do they really believe that?" Taterhead squinted at him.

Gaitlin shrugged. "I don't know, I haven't talked to them. That's just what I heard around town."

Tater sadly shook his head, then raised his eyes. "What if they *do* think I did it - like them kids say?" He took a sharp breath, fighting down tears as he implored, "What'll I do?"

After a moment Gaitlin said, "I don't know, but I'm bailing you out of here."

OTHER DREAMS

SEVEN

THREE KIDS AND A RAT

They were sitting around a small campfire in a circular clearing in the middle of Tess's Grove, a 10-acre stand of timber just north of town where the local kids often partied. But now it was a Monday night and the grove was deserted except for Erica Erickson, Johnny Bulger, Kevin Crisper and Kelsy "Bullets" O'Brien. All three kids had snuck out of their bedroom windows to be there, and now they were gathered close around the small, hissing fire, sitting cross-legged on the ground, the flickering orange light reflected in their young faces. Bullets was pacing about opposite them, the chirruping of crickets close. Somewhere an owl hooted, and from afar the distant barking of a dog echoed lonely.

At last Bullets stopped pacing and turned to face the three youngsters on the other side of the fire. "You guys really screwed up," he said with quiet disgust. "This was just supposed to be a little joke, remember? You were just supposed to grab a couple of cartons of eggs and then we were gonna egg 'em as he went under the tracks on Route 32, remember?"

The fire popped, a flurry of red sparks snaking skyward and startling all of them. They were feeling very guilty. "Well we didn't know he was gonna catch us!" Johnny Bulger whined after a moment.

"You could've just left the eggs, then!" Bullets snapped.

"We panicked," Erica said evenly, looking up at Bullets. "And the next thing we knew he was all over us, and then one thing led to another and there we were."

"Yeah, we had to do somethin'!" Kevin Crisper put in, "so we made all that up about him attackin' Erica and stuff so we wouldn't get in trouble."

"But he *did* attack me!" Erica cried with wounded indignation. "Just 'cause we took some of his lousy eggs. Big deal! He had no right to *attack* me like that."

Bullets pondered for a moment, then said, "No, I guess you're right. Not for three lousy cartons of eggs." He paused, adding, "Well, then I guess Taterhead just overreacted and got himself into the mess he's in, didn't he?"

The three adolescents nodded, Kevin adding, "Yeah, he had no right to attack Erica that way."

"You see the way I punched him out?" Johnny snickered, still crowing. "He was *cryin'!* Did you guys see that?"

"Yeah, we heard all about it," Kevin said with tired boredom.

"About 15 times today," Erica put in.

Looking stressed, Bullets began pacing again. All at once he stopped and turned. "Well, what are we gonna do about it?"

"What'a you mean?" Johnny looked at him.

But Bullets caught Erica's eye. "Can't you back off a little on your story, Erica?"

"Back off?"

"Yeah, I mean, couldn't you say after you thought about it awhile you realized he'd tore your shirt by accident, and in all the excitement you *thought* he was trying to feel you up? Something like that?"

"What about us sayin' Tater wanted to take us in the woods and get us naked?" Kevin interjected.

At that Bullets looked vexed. "I - I don't know," he stammered.

But Erica answered for all of them. "No," she quietly insisted. "If we start backing off now what'll that make *us* look like? If I start changing my story, eventually people are gonna get the idea and the truth is gonna come out and that's gonna make *me* look like the lowest, most disgusting bitch on earth. No one will ever come near me again as long as I live!" She caught her breath and looked hard at Bullets. "No," she insisted again, adamantly shaking her head. "I'm sticking with my story. I don't care what you guys say. After all, Tater got himself into this and now he's just gonna have to get himself out again."

Johnny Bulger, the hero warrior, quickly nodded. "I'm with Erica."

"So am I," Kevin Crisper said with a glance at his companions.

Throwing his hands up in defeat, Bullets heaved a sigh. "All right, if that's the way you guys want it. After all, it's easy for me, all I gotta do is keep my mouth shut. Don't forget, I wasn't even there. But you guys better make damn sure you got your stories straight before you go into that courtroom or you might come out of it looking pretty stupid."

"We already got it down this morning," Erica retorted confidently.

"Yeah," Johnny Bulger put in.

"But. . . ." Kevin's voice trailed off.

"But what?" Bullets asked irritably.

"But what if Mr. Erickson. . . does what you told us earlier? What if he's really gonna. . ." his voice trailed off again.

"Cut off his. . . ." Johnny Bulger started to say.

"He won't," Erica shook her head. "My old man was just really pissed when he said that. He'll get over it."

"Besides," Bullets intoned with a wink and a grin, "it wouldn't matter much to Taterhead. I mean, the kid's 21 and never been with a girl before. What's he ever gonna do with it besides pee, anyway? And for that the doctor can always sew on a rubber one, right?"

At that the three kids burst out laughing.

But deep inside (or was it *outside?)* a little voice kept telling Bullets to change direction. To alter the course he was on and to do it immediately - before it was too late.

OTHER DREAMS

EIGHT

A MOB ACTION

It wasn't until the next day after work that Gaitlin Tyler was able to get to the bank and draw out the $500 dollars he needed to spring Taterhead. The previous evening, on his way home from visiting him at the county lockup, he'd stopped by the Ellis' and told them he intended on bailing their son out. After a lot of talking he even managed to convince a drunken Buster that maybe Taterhead wasn't so guilty after all. At least he'd gotten the man to admit that Taterhead might be innocent, regardless of what everyone in town thought. Of course Jane Ellis had been a lot easier to bring around, and by the time he left it was with her assurances that Randy could come home once Gaitlin got him out of jail.

The first thing Taterhead wanted to know as they left the county lockup and started across the parking lot for Gaitlin's car was what happened to his truck.

"I don't know," Gaitlin shrugged, sliding behind the wheel as Taterhead got in the passenger side. "It's probably still sitting in town where you left it."

Tater shook his head in disgust. "All them eggs gone to waste."

But they hadn't gone to waste. When Gaitlin pulled in next to Tater's old red Ford pickup still parked out front of

O'Brien's Grocery and Meat Market, the first thing they discovered was that the entire load was gone. And all four tires slashed. And a big rock had been heaved through the windshield where it still lay amongst the shattered glass glittering green on the seat.

Looking like he wanted to cry but fighting it, Taterhead walked 'round and 'round the truck, Gaitlin following him until at last he put a hand on his shoulder and said with quiet encouragement, "Take it easy."

It worked. Taterhead climbed the curb and stopped on the sidewalk before the front of the truck, heaved a shaky sigh and said with despair, "I don't have the money for four new tires."

"Get some used ones down at the junkyard," Gaitlin suggested. "You can get them cheap there."

"What about the windshield?"

"You got plenty of time to get that fixed before it gets cold out."

Just then Jeanette Bulger, Johnny Bulger's mother, came out of O'Brien's clutching several packages. Startled when she saw Taterhead, she stopped, looked him up and down like she was going to spit on him, said, "Pervert," and made a wide path around him to her car as if the boy had a contagious disease.

Not 30 seconds later Henry "The Weasel" Hillard's battered old green Chrysler came roaring down Main Street farting blue smoke, slowed at the sight of Gaitlin and Taterhead, and crept past with Weasel and Nervous Nate rubbernecking the two boys on the sidewalk. Up the street a block the big old Chrysler swung in at the Gray Wolf Tap where the boys got out of the car and went inside.

"My chickens!" Taterhead suddenly exclaimed. "I gotta get home and feed my chickens!"

Gaitlin could smell trouble brewing anyway and was anxious to be off. "I fed 'em for you yesterday," he said as they got in the car.

"Thanks. Guess I'll take care of the truck tomorrow."

The chickens were clucking up a storm as Taterhead, looking very dismal, moved about tossing handfuls of feed.

"All I'm saying is you can't let this get you down," Gaitlin insisted as he followed his friend around the wire mesh enclosure. "If you're innocent. . . ."

"If?" Taterhead stopped and looked at him.

Gaitlin held out his hands. "What I'm trying to say is," he looked around, momentarily at a loss for words. "What I mean is, you didn't do this thing these kids are saying and the truth'll come out in court and then your life'll go back to normal like this never happened. People'll forget all about it once you're found innocent in court."

Taterhead stared hard at his friend. At last he said bitterly, "Yeah, sure Gaitlin. I don't have any witnesses, and everybody in town is saying kids don't lie. Just how am I gonna get the court to believe *my* side a the story?"

Gaitlin expelled a big breath of air, looked up at the sky, down at the ground, and then at his friend. "I don't know, Tater, but *I* believe you, okay?"

Taterhead stuck out his lower lip in thought and slowly nodded. "Thanks, Gaitlin," he said, tossed the last of the feed, hung the bucket on a nail under the eave of the hen house, picked up the woven cane basket he used for collecting eggs, and disappeared inside the chicken coop to see what he could find.

Gaitlin moved to follow him but stopped. The chicken coop was on the far side of the barn out of view from the back of the house, but it was the distant thud of several slamming car doors that stopped him in his tracks. It sounded like a lot of people out front. Disconcerted, Gaitlin shook off the worst of his fears and followed Taterhead into the chicken coop.

"This is probably the end of my egg business, too," Taterhead said sadly as Gaitlin joined him in collecting the eggs, "since everybody in town's against me now."

Gaitlin shrugged. "Ah, so what? If that happens you'll find something else to do."

"What?" Taterhead looked at him.

"Never mind," Gaitlin answered quickly, reaching for the last egg. "Let's get up to the house." He was concerned about what was going on out front.

As they came around the barn they could hear loud voices coming from the front yard of the big old house. When Taterhead started for the side, intending to go around front, Gaitlin grabbed his arm and gently steered him for the back door. "Let's go this way and put the eggs in the fridge first."

While stowing the eggs in one of several refrigerators set up in the kitchen for just that purpose, Taterhead noted the unusual sight of the front door standing open, a rectangle of golden, rosy-hued late afternoon light glowing brightly against the blackness of the dark, dilapidated living room. It looked like the escape route out of a bad dream. Except for the voices from beyond. They sounded angry.

A cry went up as Gaitlin and Taterhead stepped out onto the porch, several people in the crowd on the front lawn shouting, "There he is! There's Taterhead now!" Buster Ellis, his wife at his side, was nervously clutching a shotgun held at the ready.

Cars and pickup trucks were scattered everywhere about the driveway and front lawn. It seemed half the town had shown up. At the front of the mob, which gleefully seemed to be enjoying it all, were Axl Erickson, Bert Crisper and his wife Suzi, Johnny Bulger's father, Ron Bulger, and Weasel, Nervous Nate, Fat Bart and Bullets.

"Well I can tell you one thing," a red-faced Axl shouted, "your kid ain't gonna get away with it! I don't care what some judge says, I will have justice!" Turning on Taterhead he held up the big hunting knife and added, "You better hope you get a long prison sentence, kid, 'cause if you don't *this'll* be waitin' for ya when ya get out!"

"You'd best be careful the crown of thorns you fashion for my son's head, because it may come down upon your own!" Jane Ellis shouted in a voice whose strength and volume shocked Taterhead. He'd never heard his mother sound so strong before. In fact she so rarely said anything at all he was almost surprised she could talk.

"We just don't want Tater out wanderin' the streets!" Ron Bulger angrily asserted, "he's dangerous. Next time he attacks some kid there may not be anyone around to help!"

Outraged, Taterhead stepped forward. Fighting back tears, he shouted in a voice trembling with emotion, "I didn't attack nobody, Mr. Bulger!"

"You callin' my little girl a liar?" Axl bellowed indignantly.

"Kids don't lie!" Several of the onlookers immediately chanted.

Ignoring the crowd and fixing on Axl, Taterhead angrily shouted, "Ya damn right I am!"

This prompted Axl to make a move for the porch, but several hands grabbed him as Buster Ellis brought the shotgun to bear and snarled, "Come on and I'll blow your goddamned head off sure as I'm standin' here!"

"You old drunk," Axl sneered, "you couldn't hit the broad side of a barn!"

"I don't need to hit a barn," Buster replied coolly, "all I gotta do is hit you, and you ain't that far away."

"Yeah, well you ain't the only one in this town with a gun, just remember that. And you, Gaitlin," Axl suddenly directed his attention at the Tyler boy and continued in his best John Wayne imitation, "you're the one that bailed him out, and if he hurts another kid I'm not going to the sheriff, the deputy, or the state police, I'm comin' to you!"

"Now just a minute, Mr. Erickson," Gaitlin said through tightly controlled anger. "What if you're wrong? What if all this is merely about a couple of kids pulling a prank and when they got caught, they got scared and made up a big lie to hide their own wrong doing?" He paused for a moment. "Would that be such a strange thing for a 13-year-old to do? Would it? Heck, Taterhead's practically still a kid himself. But he's an honest one, and everybody knows it. And *I* know Taterhead didn't do anything but chase down some kids stealin' eggs off his truck, and that's all this amounts to."

"Put a lid on it, Gaitlin!" someone in the crowd shouted.

"How the hell would you know?" someone else shouted, "were you there?"

"Maybe it's time for a little frontier justice! Gaitlin don't give a damn what happened to my daughter! None of 'em do!" Axl cried, releasing the floodgates of pandemonium as clenched fists rose in the air along with whooping war cries and jeering shouts.

Suddenly the mob was surging and undulating like a writhing monster trying to break free, those in back screaming for vengeance and shoving forward, while those in front beneath the ominous barrel of the shotgun Buster was wildly waving back and forth struggled to hold them back.

"Get in the house, lock the doors and call the police!" Buster cried over his shoulder. When his wife and the two boys hesitated he shouted, "Now move!"

But before they could the wailing siren and flashing red lights of a Jefferson County squad car intruded, tires squealing and engine roaring as it whipped off the blacktop and skidded to a stop in the driveway.

Leaping from the vehicle, Hal Rankin raised his shotgun to the sky but hesitated. His mere appearance on the scene had quieted the angry mob. Lowering the shotgun, he announced in a loud voice, "I don't know what you all think you're doin' here, but I could arrest every one of you for trespassing and mob action. Now move out before I do, and don't come back!"

There was a long silence with much murmuring before Axl stepped forward. "Taterhead's out on the streets again and we don't like it!" he exclaimed to indignant shouts of support from the crowd.

"Well he posted bail and he is out and that's that!" Rankin declared, abruptly cocking the shotgun. "So clear out and be quick about it!"

Again a murmur spread through the crowd. The pit of his stomach aflutter, Rankin feared he might have a bigger problem than he first thought and was about to take a step back when the crowd started breaking up and heading for their vehicles. Taking a disgruntled Axl by the arms, Ron Bulger and Bert Crisper urged him along to his glowing, brand new candy-apple-red Chevy four-wheel-drive pickup.

With vehicle doors slamming and engines starting up, the Ellis's and Gaitlin stood silently on the porch watching in the fading light of an August sunset. Buster held his shotgun in a loose grip now, the barrel pointing down at the porch boards.

As some of the townsfolk went by, Rankin tried a little public relations, giving a nod here or a comment there such as, "Drive safe now," but no one seemed to notice as they grimly brushed past on the way to their vehicles.

Before the last car pulled out, Rankin, still carrying his shotgun loosely in one hand, crossed the lawn to the porch and stopped before Buster. "Seems you got a bit of a problem," he said, looking up at the watery-eyed grizzled old farmer.

The frightening experience of being the focal point of a mob action having sobered Buster up considerably, he paused a moment before replying, "I'm sure glad you got here when you did, but how'd you know?"

"George Tyler was driving home from work, saw what was going on and gave me a call."

"Thank God!" Mrs Ellis declared in a trembling voice.

"What are you going to do about this, sir?" Gaitlin asked rather pointedly.

Rankin thought for a moment, then looked at him and shrugged, replying sincerely, "I don't know, got any suggestions?"

Gaitlin stared at him blankly.

"They can't come here like that," Taterhead interjected, "it ain't right."

"They know that," Rankin replied, "and that's why they left."

"But what if they come back?" Mrs. Ellis asked worriedly.

"Oh, I don't think you have to worry about that, Jane," Rankin soothed. "They're all on their way home now, gettin' ready to settle in for the evening. They know it's over."

"For now," Buster said gravely.

"I don't think you have much to worry about at this point," Rankin turned to him reassuringly. "When they're all in a crowd like that they tend to heat each other up, but once they get away from each other, and work and life gets back to normal, I don't think anyone's gonna do anything to anyone on a person-to-person basis."

"Well I hope not," is all Buster could think to say.

"We've lived here all of our lives!" Mrs. Ellis exclaimed, a certain strength returning to her voice that Taterhead duly noted for the second time that evening. "What's wrong with these people?"

Rankin looked down, touching the brim of his big Stetson briefly, then looked up again. "Times are changin', Jane," he said. "People are sick of the violence in the streets and vicious criminals getting released back into the community by judges or overcrowded prisons. It's a bad time to be accused of anything."

"But Randy said them kids was stealin' eggs off his truck. How come they didn't get arrested for *that?*" Buster wanted to know.

Rankin shrugged. "I can take a report and file charges of petty theft if you want," he paused. "But I don't think it would be in your best interest."

"Why not?" Taterhead asked.

Rankin turned to him. "Well, to tell you the truth, son, what good would it do? First of all, it would be three kids' word against yours, and in the end all the judge is gonna do is tell them not to do it again, which those kids know well enough in the first place. So if you press charges, really all you're gonna get out of it is a town full of people angrier at you than they already are."

After a long silence Gaitlin glanced at Taterhead. "He's right. Might as well just save it and tell your side in court."

Eyes downcast, Taterhead nodded.

Swinging the shotgun onto his shoulder and casually draping a hand over the barrel, Rankin asked by way of preparing to leave, "You folks okay, now?"

Buster nodded. "Guess so."

"Like I said, I don't think you'll be having any more trouble. Just the same," he turned to Mrs. Ellis, "I will be keepin' an eye on your place. And," he hastened to add, "if you even *suspect* some kind of trouble is brewin' call right away. Don't wait. If it turns out to be a false alarm that's okay, I'll understand. I'd rather come here once or twice for nothin' than get here too late and find a tragedy, know what I mean?"

OTHER DREAMS

NINE

LOSING GROUND

"Look," Taterhead said, pulling the crumpled Bazooka comic from his pocket as Gaitlin wheeled the pickup around the corner onto Main Street. Work was called because of rain, so Gaitlin borrowed his dad's pickup and volunteered to help Taterhead get tires on his truck. On the way to the junkyard they decided to take a pass through town and see how Taterhead's truck was doing.

"Go ahead, look," Taterhead said, holding the shiny bit of colored paper out.

"I don't need to look," Gaitlin said, eyeballing Taterhead's red Ford as they drove by. "Yep, still there."

"I read this just before I went outside and caught them kids stealin' my eggs," Taterhead insisted. "And it came true, just like the fortune said, almost word for word. Look." He held the bit of paper out again.

"Okay, what's it say?" an exasperated Gaitlin asked.

"It says," Taterhead began, holding the comic up with a great flourish, *"Unexpected detour lies ahead!"* He turned to Gaitlin. "See?"

"See what?" Gaitlin asked irritably as he made the county blacktop and turned south.

"Well, the fortune," Taterhead answered matter-of-factly. "No sooner had I read it than I went outside and it came true, word for word. Detour's the understatement of the year! I mean, I didn't even get to finish my route!"

"Give me a break, Tater. That fortune could apply to a million different distractions that might've come up just after you read it." Then he added, "Sometimes I can't believe how simple-minded you are!"

"But it's happened before!" Taterhead protested, admitting, "maybe they don't work for everyone, but they do for me!"

Gaitlin shook his head. "You're goofy if you think the fortune in a bubble gum wrapper applies specifically to you. And don't tell anyone else about this," he added, "or maybe they *will* lock you up!"

"Fine," Taterhead said, folding his arms across his chest and remaining silent for the rest of the trip to Jed's Junkyard and Salvage. But not before safely tucking the comic in his pocket. Later it would be returned to his collection of other Bazooka comics whose fortunes had come true.

"Hi, Jed," Gaitlin cheerfully greeted the man as he and Taterhead walked through the door of the plain, rectangular concrete block building, the yard beyond entirely enclosed by a 10-foot-tall steel fence.

Sitting on a stool behind the tall counter that divided the room, Jed Holiday looked up from the starter motor he was working on. "Hi, boys," he smiled. He did a double take when he noticed Taterhead. "Thought you was in jail for rapin' Erica Erickson, Tater," he commented, leaning over the electrical device with a small screwdriver to make an adjustment.

Taterhead just looked at him dumbfounded.

"Raping her!" Gaitlin exclaimed.

"That's what I heard. Right in the middle of Main Street. Sowin' your wild oats, eh?" he chuckled, glancing up at Taterhead briefly while he worked.

"I didn't do no such thing!" Taterhead retorted indignantly, "and I don't even wanna know who told you that 'cause they're full a shit!"

"Sorry, Tater, I'm just tellin' ya what I heard."

"Yeah, well ya heard wrong!" he snapped, "and I'm tired of bein' falsely accused just 'cause some kids got caught stealin' my eggs!"

"That what it's all about?" Jed stopped working and looked up. "I didn't hear nothin' 'bout that before."

"Yeah, well it's the damn truth!" Gaitlin angrily declared.

Jed shrugged noncommittally. "Well don't get mad at me, what'a I know? Only what I hear."

"Well you just heard a different version of what happened," Gaitlin put in, "you gonna spread *that* around, too?"

Jed laid his screwdriver down. "Now look, if you boys came in here lookin' for a fight, go somewhere else. I got work to do."

All at once embarrassed, Gaitlin dropped his aggressive stance. "Sorry, Jed," he said apologetically. "Didn't mean to be rude, but there's a lot of trouble brewing over this and it's starting to get out of hand."

"Fair enough," Jed said, his tone becoming businesslike as he asked, "so what can I do for you boys?"

"I need four 15-inch tires for my truck," Taterhead spoke up. "Cheap ones if you got 'em."

Rolling off his stool with a groan and creaking knees, Jed said, "I might have just what you're looking for, c'mon."

Gaitlin and Taterhead came around the side of the counter and followed him through a door to the back room.

The boys picked out four tires, paid $20 dollars apiece for them and loaded them into the back of the pickup.

"See ya, Jed," Gaitlin called, getting into the truck.

"Yeah, bye," Taterhead called, getting in the other side and slamming the door.

Working slowly in a light, misting rain with a single jack and lug wrench, it took the boys over an hour to get the wheels off, the old tires removed and the new ones mounted at the Tyler's service station, and then remounted on the truck. Still, it was only 10:30 by the time they finished.

"Let's get back up to your house, load up the truck and see if we can't get some deliveries in yet this morning," Gaitlin suggested, adding, "I'll go with you." In light of all that had happened he suspected that Taterhead might be afraid to go out alone, and the quicker he got his friend back into his old routine, Gaitlin felt, the better for all, including everyone in town.

Finished tightening the last lug nut, Taterhead dropped the wrench to the pavement with a ringing clatter and stood up. "Would you?" he asked, blinking his blue eyes.

"Sure," Gaitlin replied easily, shoved his glasses back on his nose and added, "I always wondered what it would be like to have a delivery route like you anyway."

"Thanks, Gaitlin," Taterhead said gratefully.

"No problem," Gaitlin replied, picking up the jack and lug wrench and tossing them in the back of Taterhead's truck. "I'll follow you up to your house."

In no time they cartoned off and loaded up the eggs, and by 11:30 set off down the Birchwood Blacktop for town in Taterhead's rattly old pickup, the greenish glitter of shattered windshield glass littering the dirty rubber mats on the floor.

"I'll wait here and watch the eggs," Gaitlin volunteered when they pulled up out front of O'Brien's Grocery and Meat Market.

"Thanks," Taterhead said, climbing out of the truck. "Back in a minute."

He loaded up the eight cartons Mrs. O'Brien usually required and went into the store, the familiar tinkling of the little attached bell sounding like a warm greeting from an old friend.

Mrs. O'Brien happened to be behind the counter when he came in. She looked up and immediately her face fell. "Oh. Tater. I'm sorry. I probably should have called, but really, I didn't think you'd be back in business so soon after. . ." her voice trailed off.

She took a moment to smooth down the familiar, white, beef-stained apron, then continued apologetically, "I really didn't know when you'd be back. I mean, for two whole days, three if you count this morning, I didn't see or hear a word from you." She shrugged. "I couldn't go without eggs for my customers so I had to call another supplier."

Taterhead just stood there, his heart sinking like a stone.

"I hope you understand," she added as the silence grew thick. "I simply had no choice."

At last Taterhead ventured meekly, "What about tomorrow?"

Mrs. O'Brien tightened her lower lip. "Hmmm. . . the problem is," she offered after a thoughtful moment, "the other supplier is already scheduled to come out tomorrow. In fact I've already got an arrangement all worked out with them and I don't want to turn around and just drop them the next day for no apparent reason because then, well, if something were to happen to you they might not come so quick the next time I called, know what I mean? But let's see how things go," she hastily added, "and maybe sometime down the road when all this trouble is settled we can make some arrangement again, okay?" She forced a smile and quickly nodded her head as if demonstrating for Tater the proper response.

"But Mrs. O'Brien. . ." Taterhead began.

"I'm sorry, Tater, really I am, but as I've just explained, I already have other arrangements for the time being. As for the future, we'll just have to see. I really did like doing business with you, Tater. The service, the price, and the product were good and you were close by, too. Maybe we'll see, okay?"

The price of eggs just went up in Harlot. And so had Mrs. O'Brien's trade, as customers that Taterhead normally would have serviced over the last two days had already come in for their eggs. What the heck, it was only a quarter more per carton.

Taterhead nodded glumly. "Okay, Mrs. O'Brien. Call if you need me, I'll still be around."

"Sure you will, Tater," she assured him in a tone that made him feel she wasn't at all sure he would still be around - at least not for very much longer.

"What happened?" Gaitlin asked as soon as Taterhead returned lugging the cartons.

"Said she got another supplier," he answered as he loaded the cartons into the truck bed.

"Oh."

Three customers and three more turn-downs later, including a rejection from Rachel at Rachel's Cafe (she too had signed with the supplier O'Brien's had contracted with), Gaitlin had to coax strenuously to get Taterhead to go for a fourth try.

By the time Taterhead dejectedly returned to the truck from his fourth failed delivery attempt, the sun broke through the clouds and patches of blue began showing.

"See?" Taterhead almost wailed as he dropped despairingly behind the wheel, "nobody wants to buy my eggs anymore! My business is ruined 'cause a them kids!"

"Whew! It sure got hot and humid all of a sudden!" Gaitlin exclaimed, taking off his glasses and wiping sweat from his brow with a forearm. "Look, the sun came out."

"Big deal."

"Hey Tater?" Gaitlin inquired, putting his glasses back on.

"Yeah?"

"Let's say to heck with it for today and go for a swim down at Schlockrod's pond." When Taterhead didn't respond he implored, "Come on, what'a you say?"

After a silent moment Taterhead lifted a shoulder. "I guess so."

"Good. Let's. I don't think I've been swimming all summer."

*   *   *

"Boy, you just can't trust anybody anymore," Taterhead commented as he pulled out onto the blacktop and headed for the swimming hole abandoned along the tracks by the railroad when they built the roadbed some 150 years ago.

"You can say that again," Gaitlin readily agreed, "not even Rock-n-Roll."

"What'a you mean?" Taterhead asked as he slowed the truck, down-shifted and turned into the tire tracks worn through the weeds that ran along the rails to the pond.

"I was up at the mall in Rockford one day and stopped in the rock shop. I'm checking out one of *Boston's* albums and in the liner notes it says that certain proceeds from the album will go to these goofy animal rights activists."

"You gotta be kiddin' me!" Taterhead exclaimed.

Gaitlin shook his head. "All of a sudden their songs don't sound so good anymore. At least not to me."

"Yeah," Taterhead looked at him and raised a shoulder, "who wants to buy an album from a band that's givin' money to fruitcakes who wreck scientific labs to rescue mice?"

"Which reminds me," Gaitlin interjected, "autumn's just around the corner and I need to get a new set of mouse traps, the old ones are getting pretty yuckey. You can only crush so many mouse heads before the traps start getting nasty, know what I mean?"

"Get some cats," Taterhead suggested as he pulled into the brush a little ways and switched off the ignition. How the small two-acre body of water secluded by an overgrowth of brush and trees came to be called "Schlockrod's Pond" was anybody's guess. There were no Schlockrod's living in Harlot, and never had been as far as anyone knew.

"I don't have my shorts with me," Taterhead said with the sudden realization that he had nothing to swim in.

Gaitlin was wearing his. "So what?" he shrugged, "I seen you before - go skinny dipping."

"Uh-uh," Tater firmly shook his head. "Not unless you do, too."

Gaitlin looked at him. "Okay," he shrugged after a moment, "no big deal. Besides," he pointed out with a grin, "it might feel good."

They climbed out of the truck and stripped down, each on his own side, and tossed their clothes in back.

"Last one in's a rotten egg!" Gaitlin called across the back of the truck.

"Hey, no fair!" Taterhead protested, "you're closer to the water." And then he bolted around the back of the truck.

Gaitlin hesitated just long enough to give him the lead, then both boys raced naked down the footpath to the water where Gaitlin skidded to a stop and took off his glasses. Taterhead dived right in and burst to the surface with fists in the air, shouting, "I won! I won!"

Carefully setting his glasses in the crotch of a big old cottonwood on the bank, Gaitlin proclaimed with a laugh, "Fair and square, too!"

For almost an hour the boys splashed around in the pond, engaging in at least one water fight, with both boys steadfastly claiming victory. Afterwards they turned to the knotted rope hung from the thickest branch of the cottonwood and repeatedly swung out over the water and dropped in to see who could make the biggest cannonball splash or do the most outrageous back-flip.

By the time they climbed from the water, made refreshingly cool from the light rain earlier in the day, the sun was high and hot. Gaitlin grabbed his glasses and then they started along the dirt path back to the truck, the droplets clinging to their naked bodies sparkling in the golden light of late afternoon, while a warm, tingling breeze sensually dried them.

"Skinny dipping does feel good, don't it?" Taterhead grinned as they reached the truck.

"Yeah it does," Gaitlin agreed as Taterhead went around the front, pulled the squeaky door open and climbed behind the wheel.

Gaitlin hesitated by the passenger door. "What're you doing?" he asked, one hand on the door handle.

"Get in, get in," Taterhead gestured impatiently.

Cocking his head in a questioning manner, Gaitlin pulled the door open and climbed in.

"Don't it feel weird sittin' in the truck naked?" Taterhead grinned.

Gaitlin laughed and shook his head, admitting, "Yeah, but it's *supposed* to feel weird. I mean, when's the last time you drove somewhere naked?"

"Did you ever sit in your car naked?"

Again Gaitlin shook his head. "No. Do you always get this silly even before beer?"

Grinning, Taterhead nodded, saying, "Hey, let's go get some."

"Sounds good to me," Gaitlin answered as both boys simultaneously popped their doors open and swung out of the truck to get dressed.

Like deer at night caught in a car's headlights, both boys froze in their tracks, staring as Weasel's battered old Chrysler, a big green dinosaur of a car from yesteryear, quietly coasted to a stop behind Taterhead's pickup. Nervous Nate and Fat Bart turned to each other in giddy delight and exclaimed in unison, "Tater and Gaitlin are homos!" Leaning half out the windows with hoots and jeers, they hollered, "Fuckin' queers! Wait'll everyone hears about this!"

By now Gaitlin and Taterhead, burning with shame, were dressing as quickly as possible, Taterhead so nervous he kept stepping on his underwear and knocking them to the ground each time he tried to stick a foot through.

"Fuckin' homos!" Weasel yelled out the window as he restarted the big V-8 engine. Turning to his companions he breathlessly exclaimed, "Let's get out of here before someone else comes along and thinks we're with *them.*" Fat Bart and Nervous readily agreed and the big green Chrysler roared off, raising a trail of dust all the way to the blacktop.

"Boy, wait'll everyone hears about this!" Fat Bart crowed.

"If they'd been swimming or something that'd be different," Nervous Nate put in, "but they were sittin' buck naked in Tater's truck - together," he paused, "now *that's* queerin'-off!"

"As queer as you can get!" Fat Bart chuckled as Weasel hit the blacktop and turned towards town with tires screeching and engine roaring.

Within the hour heads were nodding and tongues wagging all over town as the rumor took flight even faster than the one of Taterhead's supposed sexual attack on Erica Erickson. And all agreed that two grown men caught naked together in the cab of a truck was two grown men caught queerin'-off.

At the Gray Wolf Tap Bullets took a swig of beer and drawled, "No tellin' what Tater's been doin' to those eggs he's been deliverin' all over town."

"Yeah, and how many did *you* eat?" someone asked
Bullets blanched.

The thought that Taterhead might have been deliberately spreading AIDS around town gripped everyone with fear. After all, he'd been pegged as a weirdo for years, although people had been too polite to say anything. At that time, though, no one had an inkling the extent of his weirdness. That he was slow, emotionally unbalanced, predisposed to sexual violence, *and* a homosexual - now that was a horse of a different color. And Gaitlin! Who would have ever suspected Gaitlin Tyler of being queer?

As the hysteria mounted some immediately turned to the phone to make arrangements for AIDS testing. Others turned to murderous thoughts. And everyone remembered the bloody scratch on Erica's breast, caused, supposedly, by Taterhead's fingernail when he tried feeling her up. Poor Erica. Could the AIDS virus be transferred that way?

"Well, it broke the skin," someone pointed out.

"To hell with the knife," Axl Erickson said, standing up so fast his bar stool toppled to the floor with a loud *bang*.

"Where're you goin'?" Lowell Boredwith asked as Axl headed for the door without bothering to pick up the stool.

Halfway to the exit Axl stopped and turned. "To get my gun," he said, looking the man up and down as if expecting a challenge. "Queerin'-off's illegal in this state and it's time someone hunted them two homos down and brought 'em in. After all, he might'a infected my daughter when he attacked her, and I ain't takin' the chance a them two escapin', 'cause one thing's for sure, now that they been caught red-handed and know that *we* know they're queer they might try and make a run for it."

Pandemonium immediately broke out, half the afternoon crowd loudly clamoring to go along and gallantly offering Axl their assistance, while the other half noisily egged them on. And before he knew it Lowell Bordewith found himself alone as the whole place emptied out into the street.

Sadly shaking his head, he came around the bar to pick up the overturned stool. He was disappointed because he wanted to go too. He always missed the good stuff. But then, there was no way he could close the place up on a Thursday afternoon. He had one consoling thought, though. At least if any stragglers stopped by he'd have the fun of telling them the latest news about Gaitlin Tyler and Taterhead Ellis. Homos.

OTHER DREAMS

TEN

NO TEARS FOR QUEERS

Hal Rankin happened to be sitting in his patrol car on the hill in the church parking lot when the afternoon crowd at the Gray Wolf Tap emptied into the street and excitedly scrambled for their cars. Instinctively he knew it probably had something to do with Taterhead Ellis and immediately fired up the engine and pulled out.

Roaring down Main Street, he swung over to the side out front of the tavern and screeched to a stop, blocking Axl just as the man started to back out of the angular stall at the curb. Hitting the strobe lights, Rankin climbed out of the squad car. "All right, everyone," he shouted, "shut your engines off and stay where you are!"

Flipping the ignition off, Axl flung the door open and angrily swung out of his pickup. "Just what the hell's goin' on, Rankin?" he fumed, strutting up to the man and stopping toe-to-toe with hands on hips.

"I was just about to ask you the same thing," the big old officer rejoined pleasantly. Turning to the crowd at large he asked loudly, "Where's everybody hurrying off to so suddenly this afternoon? Havin' a party and you didn't invite me? That hurts my feelings."

"Look, Rankin. . . ."

"No, you look, Axl," Rankin sharply interjected, "back up two steps and shut your mouth before I bust your ass for DUI."

"Easy, Axl," Bullets said, stepping out of the crowd and delicately defusing the situation by backing Axl up enough to placate Rankin.

With a glance at Bullets, Rankin turned back to Axl, saying disgustedly, "I don't know what's gotten into you, Axl, but this whole thing about a couple of kids fightin' is getting way out of hand."

"Obviously you haven't heard the latest," Bullets quickly put in.

"Oh yeah?" Rankin turned on him cynically, "and what's the latest, Bullets?"

All at once the Weasel, Fat Bart, and Nervous Nate came forward. It was the Weasel who spoke. "We caught Gaitlin Tyler and Taterhead Ellis queerin'-off down by Schlockrod's pond this afternoon."

"Gaitlin?" Rankin squinted at the boy. "And Tater?" After a moment he shook his head. "Nahhh. I don't believe it."

"It's true," Weasel insisted. "When we were comin' down the path in my car we spotted Tater's truck. I shut my engine off and just rolled up behind 'em real quiet. They didn't even know we were there."

"That's right, sir," Nervous put in, "and they both had their heads down."

Fat Bart nodded. "Yeah they did. All three of us saw it." The other two boys quickly nodded in agreement.

Rankin looked at them incredulously, then exploded, "So what!? They're settin' in Tater's truck lookin' *down* and that makes 'em queer?" He looked around the ring of excited faces that surrounded him.

"Like I said, sir, they didn't hear us come rollin' up behind 'em," Weasel carefully went on, "and just as we did they both suddenly raised their heads and jumped out of the truck before they knew we were there."   He couldn't hold back a snicker before concluding triumphantly,   "And they were both buck naked!"

"I wished we'd had a camera to take a picture,"   Fat Bart commented.

"Honest, sir, we ain't lyin' either,"   Nervous Nate put in with big, sincere eyes that he held fastened on the officer's.

Rankin held the young man's gaze and waited for him to blink.   He didn't.   During nearly 40 years with the county police force he'd looked into a lot of lying eyes, and if this kid wasn't telling the truth he'd be damned.   Still, he thought he'd better give the kid another chance to falter.   "You sure you're not stretchin' the truth a bit, son?"   he asked, keeping his eyes locked on the boy.

"No sir,"   Nervous Nate held the man's gaze.   "It's just like Weasel said, when we rolled up behind their truck they both jumped out buck naked.   Just as naked as the day they were born!"

Dropping his gaze, Rankin turned introspective for a moment.   "Hmph!"   he said to himself with a slight shake of his head.   "I never would'a thought Gaitlin. . ."   his voice trailed off.

"And just think about this,"   Bullets quickly moved in, capturing center stage,   "'cause I seen you eatin' eggs up at Rachel's plenty of times."

"So?"   Rankin looked at him.

"So where do ya suppose those eggs came from? Taterhead Ellis!"   He answered his own question.   "Now you and everybody else has known for years that Taterhead ain't too bright. . . ."

"And not very clean, neither,"   Axl interjected.

"Right!"   Bullets went on breathlessly,   "So if he's been queerin'-off with Gaitlin for who the hell knows how long, well he's probably been meetin' other queers over the years, too - hell they *both* probably got AIDS!"

Rankin opened his mouth to say something but Bullets swiftly headed him off. "Now imagine one time these two are queerin'-off together, ya know, an' when they're done Tater wipes his hands off on a rag or somethin', but maybe he's still got some a that, uh, *bodily fluids* stuck under his fingernails or somethin'. And then he delivers the eggs to Rachel's and maybe just a tiny bit, like an amount you'd need a microscope to see, gets on an egg carton. And then Rachel takes the carton and a tiny bit gets on her finger. Then, when she's bringing *your* eggs to you, maybe one almost slips off the plate and on impulse she catches it with the tip of her finger, slips the egg back on the plate, gives it to you and you start eatin' 'em!" Bullets watched the man a moment, letting it all sink in. "Get my drift, Mr. Rankin?" he asked with a grin. "Maybe you should go home and make an appointment with your doctor to get tested right away, eh?"

With Rankin suddenly looking rather worried, everyone laughed, albeit a bit nervously. (They'd eaten breakfast at Rachel's plenty of times themselves.)

Gaitlin Tyler and Taterhead Ellis? Although the thought of getting AIDS in the manner Bullets described had initially frightened him, Rankin was smart enough to realize it was a ploy to distract him from the issue at hand. Furthermore, it suddenly occurred to him, there wasn't a chance in hell of him actually contracting AIDS from some egg Taterhead had handled - even if Tater *did* have the disease.

"Well that's a very interesting theory, Bullets," Rankin said loudly, pulling himself together. "But what I want to know is, what do you boys plan to do about it?"

"Now that those two know that *we* know they're a couple of queers," Axl broke in, "well, it makes sense they might try to run. I mean, what if Tater infected my daughter when he scratched her the other day? So we was figurin', since you weren't around at the time, that we'd go make us a little citizen's arrest and hustle them boys down to the hospital and get 'em tested."

"First of all, you can't do that," Rankin began patiently. "It's against the law."

"But queerin'-off in public is against the law," Bullets interjected, "and we got three witnesses that caught 'em red-handed!"

"Well. . . ." Rankin moved his head around like it was attached to his shoulders on a spring. "I guess I could arrest them for committing sodomy in public, but I don't think the law allows us to force an AIDS test on anyone - least ways not at this point. That would be for a court to decide."

"Well we got three witnesses," Axl reiterated, "the bible only requires two, so you gonna do anything about them sodomizin' in public or what?"

Letting out a long stream of air, Rankin put his hands on his hips and looked down at his shoes. Shaking his head in wonder he said almost to himself, "I just can't believe it. . . ."

"Well it's true," Fat Bart piped up. "I was there when their heads popped up and they jumped buck naked out of that truck!"

"I was there, too," Weasel put in.

"So was I," Nervous Nate volunteered with a sharp nod. "They're as queer as a couple a three-dollar bills!"

"You boys'll have to file a complaint if I'm gonna arrest them," Rankin said gruffly, looking at the three of them.

"No problem," the three replied in perfect unison, which brought a chuckle from the crowd.

Feeling sick at heart and completely unsure of the whole thing, Hal Rankin realized he just might have to arrest Gaitlin and Taterhead on sodomy charges.

OTHER DREAMS

ELEVEN

REPRIEVE FOR THE INNOCENT

They were sitting behind the barn in Taterhead's pickup. Too scared to feed the chickens. Too scared to get out of the truck. Too scared to move.

"Damn you, anyway!" Gaitlin suddenly spat. "If we'd just gotten dressed as soon as we got back to the truck this wouldn't have happened. But Nooo, *you* had to see what it felt like to sit naked in the truck! Moron!" he scowled.

"Look who's talkin'!" Taterhead turned on him with equal anger. "You're the one that wanted to go skinny dippin', not me! Now my egg business is gone for sure!"

"Your egg business!" Gaitlin sneered. "This whole town thinks we're a couple of homos by now and all you can think about is your egg business! Don't you ever think about anything else? Don't you have any other dreams besides your damn egg business?"

Taterhead looked at him indignantly for several moments. "Yeah, I got other dreams. I was thinkin' about maybe gettin' a cow or two and addin' fresh whole milk to my product line, and maybe learnin' how to make cheese or somethin'!"

"Yeah, well you better start thinking about doing it someplace else, brother, 'cause we're both finished in this town now," Gaitlin said bitterly, whipping off his glasses and massaging his forehead.

At this point Taterhead was near tears. Suddenly he turned to Gaitlin. "Maybe we should run away. Go to California or someplace."

"Yeah, and then what?" Gaitlin looked at him as he wiped the lenses with his shirttail and put his glasses back on.

"I don't know," Taterhead shrugged, "but since we got caught there's no point stayin' around here."

At the word "caught" Gaitlin jerked imperceptibly. "You know, that's the thing, Tater, what did we get caught *doing?* Nothing!" he exploded. "And they got us so screwed up we're sitting here like we've done some great crime or something. As if we actually *were* queerin'-off!"

"It don't matter," Taterhead countered, "they're gonna *think* we were no matter what we say."

Gaitlin shook his head. "I don't care," he said firmly, "the only thing we have to worry about is what we *are,* not what they *think* we are!"

"Yeah, but. . . ."

"Yeah but nothin'!" Gaitlin countered fiercely. "You can do what you want, but I'm not letting a bunch of morons run me off. I'm stickin'. And if I have to fight every one of them single-handedly then I'll fight, but I'm not runnin' anyplace!"

*   *   *

When Hal Rankin showed up at the Ellis' back door he didn't say anything about why he had come, but merely inquired as to the whereabouts of Tater. . . er, Randy.

"Yes," Jane Ellis nodded, watching the officer closely, "him and Gaitlin just pulled up a few minutes ago. I saw Randy's truck. They must be out back feedin' the chickens."

"Thank you, ma'am," Rankin said, offering a slight nod as he touched the brim of his big brown Stetson and turned to leave.

"Is anything the matter, Mr. Rankin?" Jane Ellis asked in a small, concerned voice.

Turning back, Rankin paused, then answered sincerely, "I'm not sure yet, ma'am. I just want to talk to the boys for a minute if that's okay."

"Certainly, certainly," she answered, "you just go right ahead, I'm sure they're out back."

"Thank you, ma'am," he said, again touched the brim of his hat and turned to leave. He heard the door close behind him as he thumped down the back porch steps and headed across the yard.

Rounding the corner of the barn, he saw the two boys sitting in the truck and instinctively ducked back, his heart pounding. Since they were facing the other way they hadn't seen him. But what was he going to say? What would *they* say? Well, he had to find out. He took a deep breath, rounded the corner and quietly approached the truck from behind. "Hello, Tater," he said casually as he strolled up to the driver's side window.

His heart leaping in his chest, Taterhead almost jumped out of his skin. His next sensation was nauseousness. Fighting down the urge to puke, beads of sweat broke out on his forehead and he started gulping air.

Gaitlin just stared at the dashboard with unseeing eyes. For a moment talking about fighting had been very inspiring, but now he felt sick too. All he really wanted was to crawl under a rock and die.

"Can I talk to you boys for a moment?" Rankin gently asked.

With his breathing stabilized and the nauseousness fading, Taterhead stared straight ahead and slowly nodded.

"Were you boys down at Schlockrod's pond this afternoon?"

Again Taterhead nodded.

"What were you boys doing down there?"

"Swimming," Gaitlin answered vacantly, still staring at the dashboard with unseeing eyes.

"Just swimming?" Rankin asked softly.

Both boys visibly stiffened. At last Gaitlin answered, *"Just* swimming," and turned to look at the man with a level gaze.

With a little cough Rankin looked down. When he looked up again Gaitlin still held his gaze. "Some boys said. . ." he fumbled, finding no way of putting it delicately, "said they caught you queerin'-off."

Eyes still locked on the man, Gaitlin slowly shook his head. "Bullshit."

"They said you didn't know they were there and when they pulled up, the both of you jumped out of the truck. . ." Rankin paused to clear his throat, "buck naked. Is that true?"

Heaving a heavy sigh, Gaitlin looked away. "Yeah, it's true," he admitted tiredly.

"But we weren't queerin'-off!" Taterhead quickly added, his lower lip trembling as he looked at the man with eyes about to spill over with tears.

Hoping the boy wouldn't cry, Rankin asked in a tone revealing that he *wanted* to believe them, "Then what were you doing?"

"Just sittin' there!" Taterhead almost wailed.

"Waiting a minute to dry before getting dressed," Gaitlin answered softly. "And then they pulled up. . . ."

"Who?"

"Weasel and his gang."

"What'd they say to you?"

"Accused us of queerin'-off."

"And what did you boys say?"

Tater shook his head. "Nothin'. They up and left before we got a chance to say anything."

Rankin looked down again for a long, thoughtful moment. He was thinking about the police blotter and the effect it would have on these boy's lives when it appeared in print in the *Jefferson County News* that they'd been arrested on sodomy charges - even if later they were acquitted. After a moment he slapped the door edge with finality, saying, "All right," and started to turn away, but stopped short and turned back again. "Do me a favor, will ya? Don't go skinny dippin' anymore. It's illegal anyway, you know. Public indecency."

With both boys almost trembling their relief, Gaitlin managed to look up and say with a weak smile, "Thanks, sir."

Wondering just how he was going to placate Axl Erickson and the rest of them, Rankin gave the boys a tight-lipped nod, slapped the door edge again by way of saying goodbye, and crunched through the tall, dry, overgrown grass back the way he had come.

OTHER DREAMS

TWELVE

THE PLOTTING CONTINUES

There is a spiritual aspect to man that is undeniable. Sometimes we see it die, therefore it must exist. It is an aspect of the man with the womb as well as the one without, and it is the most important aspect. The aspect of any human that separates it from a cow or a pig or a rodent - the soul, which holds the spirit, which is the spark of life, a gift of God that carries on after the body dies. But sometimes a person can die spiritually, long before bodily death, and then the soul dies, dissipating the spark of life that separates man from the animals. And then he becomes one.

For Kelsy "Bullets" O'Brien this death, this evaporation of his soul, would commence without fanfare. Without his even realizing it. But it was *his* choice, a decision made within his heart and mind when he came to one pernicious conclusion - if he rejected God, or at least the *notion,* then he could make up his own rules, which would give him a distinct advantage in this life over others. Or so he believed.

Later, at the hour of his death, he could always claim ignorance and beg forgiveness. After all, hadn't Jesus himself said that if a man came seeking forgiveness, he should be forgiven seven times 70 times? As far as Bullets was concerned that equaled a lot of forgiveness coming his way.

Bullets' reasoning was gravely flawed of course. But he didn't know that. Didn't *want* to know that. Didn't want to see. Regretfully, God granted Bullets' desire. Consequently, Bullets had respect for nothing except fear. His own. The fear of being identified as a fraud. And the nagging sense that somewhere in his distant (or perhaps not so distant?) future a cold, black void empty of life had been prepared especially for him. Nevertheless, he was sucked along into the dilemma of his own creation. Blinded by his own desire for blindness.

But the only thing on Bullets' mind as he sat swigging beer with Nervous Nate Naumann and Fat Bart Binks was Taterhead Ellis. Quite often it is the fear of one's own misdeeds being disclosed that motivates a person to socially assassinate another. A violence that is all the more diabolical because of its gutlessness. For it is usually conducted behind closed doors with secret intimations that do not confront the accused and thus denies him an opportunity to defend himself.

Bullets was engaged in just such a character assassination, with quiet asides and snide remarks, when Weasel burst into the Gray Wolf and slipped into the booth with them. "I just saw Hal Rankin in town," he said excitedly.

"Did he have Gaitlin and Tater with him?" Fat Bart asked, sliding over to make room.

"No," Weasel shook his head.

"Weil what'd he say?" Nervous Nate asked. He was sitting next to Bullets on the other side of the table.

Weasel opened his mouth to answer but hesitated as Axl Erickson and the fathers of Johnny and Kevin, Ron Bulger and Bert Crisper, slipped off their stools, came over and formed a little semicircle at the foot of the table.

"Yeah, what *did* he say?" Axl asked darkly.

Weasel looked around the close circle of faces anxiously awaiting his response, the corners of his mouth turning up in a grin that revealed his two prominent front teeth. Since it wasn't often his, he loved the center of attention when he got it. "Rankin said he wasn't going to arrest them," the rat-faced boy finally answered.

"Isn't going to arrest them?" Axl was flabbergasted.

"That's what he said. Doesn't think they did anything."

"Didn't do anything!" Bullets exclaimed, outraged.

"What'a they gotta do, kill someone!?" Axl bellowed indignantly.

When he noticed that the bar crowd had fallen silent and other ears were listening, Axl turned to the little group around the table and motioned with his hands to hold it down, saying quietly, "Let's keep this to ourselves for a minute. If we let everyone in on it, it'll be just like before and nothing will get done."

Everyone nodded knowingly, Bullets quietly suggesting, "Let's get a case of beer or two and go somewhere."

"That's a good idea," Axl said, adding generously, "you guys ante up what you can and I'll put up the rest."

As everyone pulled out a few dollars and tossed them on the table, Axl gathered them up, asking, "Where'll we go?"

"Weasel's," Nervous Nate answered, "we always party there."

Weasel rented a small house, the last on a dead end street at the edge of town, the backyard of which bordered the cornfields. It was very secluded in summer with the tall corn on every side, and it was where the gang typically gathered for Friday night beer bashes and Saturday night pot parties - when they weren't partying out at Tess's Grove.

Manfully declining offers of assistance from Bert Crisper and Ron Bulger, Axl Erickson carried both cases of beer to the picnic table in Weasel's backyard and set them down with a thud. He liked this sudden alliance with the town's bad boy party crowd. If it came down to it and he had to seek justice for his daughter himself, and right now it looked like that would be the case, having these guys on his side could come in real handy.   For alibis.   For assistance.   For you name it.

Weasel appeared at his side lugging a huge red cooler.   He set it on the grass at the foot of the table, flipped the lid up, and stood aside as Fat Bart broke two large bags of ice into it. Opening the first case, Axl started handing off bottles to the boys four at a time as they stooped to the task of loading the cooler.

One thing disturbed Axl, though.   For some reason he couldn't put his finger on, Bert Crisper and Ron Bulger somehow seemed uneasy about the whole situation.   And they could turn out to be the weak link in an otherwise perfect set-up.

Handing off the last of the bottles, all at once it came to Axl how to deal with Ron and Bert.   Little by little he'd test their reactions to his plans, first offering a relatively mild punishment for Taterhead's crime, and then working his way up to more extensive punishments, carefully watching their reactions along the way.

If they balked at all he'd simply stop short of what he *really* had in mind for Taterhead.   Then he'd hold the best for last - until after Ron and Bert were gone.   He had absolute 100% trust in the boys.   They seemed as ready and enthusiastic to draw blood as he was.   Especially Bullets, and he was their leader.

"So, it looks like Rankin's just gonna let those two little homos get away with it," Bullets said over his shoulder as he splashed gasoline on the wood Nervous Nate had neatly arranged in the fire pit in the middle of the backyard.

"Want a beer, Bullets?" Axl called, "they're ready!"

"Sure," Bullets replied, struck a match and flipped it onto the wood.   With a *whoosh!* it burst into flame, a big ball of black smoke roiling skyward.   Bullets watched for a moment, then turned and went to the table where his comrades were already sitting around swigging beer.

From where he sat at the end of the table near the cooler, Axl pulled one of the brown, long-neck bottles from the ice, popped it open and set it on the table as Bullets swung a leg over the bench and sat down opposite him.

"Rankin's not gonna do a damn thing," Axl said disgustedly, taking a swig. "And that means if we want justice we're gonna have to take care of it ourselves."

Taking a rather cautious sip of his beer, Ron Bulger said, "What about the judge?"

Everyone turned to look at him. *"What* judge?" Bullets asked as if the man had just made the world's stupidest remark.

"The judge that'll be presiding at Tater's trial. He's going to have to go before a judge for what he did to Erica."

"Ahhh," Axl waved him off disgustedly. "Just what do you think the judge is going to do to him, anyway?"

"He'll probably let him off with a slap on the wrist," Bullets volunteered.

"Yeah," Nervous Nate put in his two cents.

"No doubt," Fat Bart offered his support as well, "they always do."

"Even so," it was Bert Crisper, "shouldn't we at least wait and see what happens in court? I mean, who knows? Maybe the judge won't be as easy on him as we think."

"When's his trial, anyway?" Ron asked.

"Two weeks," Axl answered, swigging beer. "But what difference does it make anyway? The worst that can happen to him, as I understand it, is a year in jail. And that's if the judge throws the book at him!"

"Well maybe the judge *will* throw the book at him," Ron said hopefully.

"Big deal!" Axl snorted, "what's a year in jail for what he did to my daughter? Nothin'!"

"Well what'd you want, Axl?" Bert asked, "you think he should get the chair?"

"That'd be too good for him," Axl retorted indignantly. "What if he gave my daughter AIDS?"

"That's another matter entirely," Bert answered. "But before we start planning revenge for *that* shouldn't we at least wait for her test results?"

"When do you expect to get the test results back?" Nervous Nate interjected.

"She hasn't even been tested yet!" Axl fumed, "they have to wait four months until after a person's been exposed before the tests will work. But I don't care what the test results are!" he went on heatedly, "I wanna nail the bastard for what he did to my daughter whether he gave her AIDS or not! And I'm surprised at you Ron, and you too, Bert," he continued in softer tones. "I mean, he attacked your boys too, ya know."

Bert raised a shoulder, saying evenly, "Maybe. Then again, maybe it was more like Gaitlin said. You know, kids just fighting."

A long silence ensued as Axl stared at him in disbelief. "Gaitlin!" he finally snorted in disgust. "Well he's going to get his, too!"

"Gaitlin?" It was Ron. "What's he got to do with any of this? It was Tater who attacked the kids. Gaitlin had nothing to do with it."

"Nothing to do with it?" Axl belched and quickly went on, "he's been helping Taterhead ever since it happened. *He's* the one bailed Tater out, don't forget. Besides, he was caught queerin'-off with Tater, and as far as I'm concerned that makes him just as bad!"

"That's right," Fat Bart put in.

"Worse," Weasel added.

"Fuckin' Fag!" Nervous Nate spat disgustedly.

At this Ron Bulger and Bert Crisper exchanged glances. "Well, I don't know what you have in mind for Taterhead and Gaitlin exactly," Ron intoned, "but I think this whole thing is getting out of hand."

Absently peeling the label from his bottle, Bert looked up, taking in the others as he nodded agreement. "Ron's right. And I can't understand either why you want to involve Gaitlin. If he *is* queer, well that's *his* problem and I feel sorry for him. I mean, I hate fags and homo's as much as the next guy, but if mother nature don't take these two out, God will. So we should just stay out of it and let nature take its course."

"And furthermore," Ron added, "just what are we gonna do to these boys, anyway? Beat them up?"

After a long, thoughtful moment Axl raised a shoulder, replying coyly, "Something like that."

Draining his beer, Ron set the bottle down and stood up. "Well, I don't know what you guys have in mind, but I don't think I wanna know, either. Count me out."

Bert Crisper stood up too. "I'm with Ron. I just want to wash my hands of this whole affair. You guys can do what you want, just leave me out of it."

"So," Axl stood up too, as if he were going to see them to the door, "does this mean you're officially joining the other side?" the big man asked, sucking in his ample beer gut and straightening to his full height.

"If you're asking me if I'm going to go running to Rankin with the news that you guys are planning something for Tater and Gaitlin, the answer is no," Bert replied evenly, keeping his eye on Axl. "Like I said, I hate fags and homos as much as the next guy, and as far as I'm concerned the conversation we had here this evening is already forgotten."

"That's right," Ron put in. "You guys do what you think you have to do, just leave us out of it and we'll forget we ever had this talk, okay?"

Looking them up and down like they were a couple of candy asses from fairyland, at last Axl grunted his assent and sat back down. Everyone else wisely remained silent. No sense fostering resentment in someone who could later testify against you if they decided to.

And they remained silent, too, until they heard the thump of car doors slamming out front, engines starting up, and tires crunching on gravel as Ron and Bert pulled out and went their separate ways.

At last Axl looked around the table, asking, "Anybody else want out now before we get down to business?"

Bullets, Weasel, Fat Bart, and Nervous Nate all met his gaze. All declined the offer to get out while the getting was good.

"Okay, then!" Axl exclaimed boisterously, all at once his jolly old self again. "Anyone ready for another beer? Don't be shy, now. Drink up, we got plenty."

As fresh beers were passed around Bullets asked, "So what's your plan, Axl?" With a knowing gleam in his eye he added, "I know it must be something good 'cause you waited until you flushed out all the whusses."

Axl's head fell back with an appreciative laugh, then he pulled out the big 10-inch buck knife he always carried strapped to his waist, stuck it in the table top with a loud *thunk* and said dramatically, "In light of the sexual attack on my daughter, Taterhead Ellis don't need to be runnin' around loose in *our* town with that weapon he's got danglin' between his legs!"

It took a moment for what he was suggesting to sink in, and then the four boys, Harlot's bad boy party animals, were sniggering wickedly, eyes alight with sadistic glee.

*   *   *

It was quiet. Jets were making thunder overhead, but they were long and far above, the turbulence they created only a whisper barely perceived by the simple men who stood upon the ground looking up.

Tossing feed to the chickens, Taterhead Ellis was looking down. He knew his life in Harlot was over. Gaitlin Tyler didn't.

*   *   *

"Why?" George Tyler grimaced at his son. "Why would *anyone* say that about you?"

"I don't know!" Gaitlin cried, "why would they?"

"I don't know, either!" George Tyler bellowed at his son. "All I know is that I had about a dozen people stop by the station today to tell me my son was caught doin'. . . doin' homo things down by Schlockrod's Pond this afternoon with Taterhead Ellis." He paced up and down in the kitchen, then stopped and turned on his son, shouting, "Why!? If it ain't true, why're they sayin' it, Gaitlin? Why!?"

Gaitlin slumped in his chair with a sigh. Looking down at the floor with eyes unseeing he admitted, "We were skinny dippin'. *That's* why."

"Skinny dipping!" his father huffed. "What're ya nuts? With everything that's happened in the last few days, you decide to go *skinny dipping?*"

"People have done more heinous crimes," Gaitlin replied sarcastically. "There's Hitler, Idi Amin, Stalin. . . . "

"Okay, smart ass," his father said evenly, "so now what're you going to do? Between you and Tater you got the whole town in an uproar. Think you're gonna be able to make your way around here like that?"

"What do you want from me?" Gaitlin frowned, shoving his glasses back on his nose.

Heaving a sigh, his father held his hands out. "I don't know, but your mother and I have to live here, too," he said, "and you're not making it any easier right now - for anyone."

Staring at his father with a harsh look on his face, Gaitlin said, "Maybe Tater was right. Maybe we should leave."

"Leave? Leave where?"

"I don't know. Tater suggested California."

"California!" George Tyler spat disdainfully.

"Well what do you suggest?"

"I suggest you stay away from Taterhead until this thing is resolved," he replied bluntly.

"You mean that?" Gaitlin looked at him.

"Yes I mean that!"

There was a strained silence before Gaitlin said, "I can't do that."

"Why?"

"'Cause that would leave Tater all alone in the middle of this thing, and I just couldn't do that to him. He didn't do anything in the first place, dad."

"So?"

"So I can't just turn my back on him now. If. . . if I did that," Gaitlin shrugged, "I don't know what he'd do. I'm the only friend he's got right now, and I'm surprised you would even suggest that. What kind of guy would turn his back on his best friend just because things got a little rough? Would you really want me to be that kind of guy?"

His father stared at him. "No," he almost whispered, slowly shaking his head. "No, I guess I wouldn't."

"Okay then," Gaitlin said, shoving his chair back and getting up, "I'm going to bed."

OTHER DREAMS

THIRTEEN

MAD MAIDS

Renee Cooley was irritated. Or confused. Or both. Nothing seemed to make sense anymore. Rumor had it that local law enforcement wasn't going to support the MAIDS in their efforts to further restrict hours at the Gray Wolf Tap, or their demands for increased roadblocks, either. As founder and president of MAIDS (Mothers Against Intoxicated Drivers), a local group she'd started after her daughter was killed by a drunk driver, she just couldn't understand it. (Unfortunately for the poor driver, who went down on manslaughter charges, the girl had actually been a suicide case, deliberately running out in front of his car as it cruised the highway at the posted speed limit.)

In any case, now Renee Cooley was running late for the emergency session she herself had called, and trembling uncontrollably as she poured fresh water into the coffee machine. Too much caffeine. Way too much. Quarts of coffee on an empty stomach. It made her smell. It made her appear spasmodic and jerky. And as she clattered about the kitchen in frantic haste, she saw tracers; mild hallucinations, her eyes darting about as her overstimulated mind, racing with the caffeine high, repeatedly flashed signals of things that weren't there.

Glancing up from the Farm Report he was watching on television over the top of his newspaper, her husband of 23 years called loudly from the lower level of the multilevel family room/kitchen, "Just calm down!" A paper millionaire several times over through smart investment, Stuart Cooley farmed 1300 acres of some of Northern Illinois' richest cropland.

Plopping into a chair at the kitchen table, Renee brought a fist down with a loud bang. "Damn!"

"What!!?" her husband exploded, looking up from the TV again.

"My coffee!" She cried, "I can't leave without my coffee!" She had her huge 20-ounce "road" cup with the plastic, tight-fitting lid at the ready.

"Your coffee," her husband snorted. "Maybe you should switch to beer. It might calm you down some."

"Oh great!" she cried, "now my husband wants me to become an alcoholic!"

"Well if this is what coffee does to you maybe you'd be better off!"

The moment the coffee machine ceased pissing its brown fluid into the pyrex receptacle she leapt to her feet, filled the cup to the top, snapped on the plastic lid and dashed for the door.

"Get a prescription," her husband said, snapping the wrinkles from his paper and turning the page.

"For what?" she almost screamed as she skidded to a stop and turned, one hand on the doorknob.

"For downers. For Valium. For anything that'd calm you down," he said evenly, realizing with mild irritation that not only was he not getting the reading done that he wanted, but he wasn't seeing the TV, either. His wife and her frantic, caffeine-induced hysteria had entirely diverted his attention.

"Ohhh you!" she almost growled in her throat like a dog threatening attack, flung the door open and ran for the driveway and her car.

Stuart Cooley lowered his paper for a moment to listen as the engine of her Cadillac Allanté revved. A moment later the tires chirped against the asphalt drive as she dropped the little high-powered car into gear and roared off for town and Saint Christian's Church where the basement meeting would be held. Perhaps he shouldn't have bought her such a powerful car he reflected, turning back to his paper.

Renee Cooley quickly accelerated up to 70 miles-an-hour, the huge tires on the little red coupe with the monster V-8 singing on a steadily rising note against the tacky asphalt still warm from the August heat of late afternoon. With a posted speed limit of 50 MPH it was much too fast for the narrow, winding blacktop that dipped and rose with the rolling terrain. But the Allanté was a sleek, low-slung sports coupe which, along with the huge, oversized radials and tacky road surface, had excellent road-holding characteristics.

Guiding the coupe around a curve, through a valley and up over the crest of a hill, Renee noted the last light of day glowering crimson on the horizon, reached for the dash and snapped on the headlights. She never used the automatic headlight system because she didn't trust it, although it was completely trustworthy. It was just one of her little quirks.

The road ahead was unfolding rapidly before her headlights as she guided the little car around yet another curve, then the road straightened and flattened out for a half mile or so.

Glancing for her coffee cup, she grabbed it from the holder and slurped the hot, bitter liquid through the vent in the plastic lid. Trembling briefly as another charge of caffeine coursed through her brain, her eyes darted about in response to electrical impulses the optic system thought were external flashes of light.

Moving to replace the plastic cup in its holder, she missed slightly and couldn't fit it. Thus distracted, she glanced down and fitted the cup. By the time she looked up again she'd used up her half mile of straight and flat.

The pavement ahead rose and curved sharply left over the crest of a hill, but as she took her foot off the accelerator three elements combined to induce a mild hallucination; the murky, humid twilight glow; the light of the high beams of a vehicle out of sight around the curve reflecting off a tree; and her own brain's neuron system highly charged with caffeine and excitedly and erratically firing off electrical impulses.

For one brief moment, for perhaps two seconds and 300 feet of distance travelled, she saw a flash of light that wasn't there and swerved to miss a vehicle she had yet to reach and wasn't in her lane to begin with, and swept around the curve - only three feet too far to the left. And that put her directly in the path of Jed Holiday's pickup truck.

Jed knew his limits. He'd been stopped once and brought to the station for a breathelizer test. Four beers in the belly found him under the 0.10 limit that determines legal intoxication - but just barely. The police officer warned him that he was playing with fire and let him go.

On his way north to deliver a machine part to an old friend and valued customer, he'd stopped in at the Gray Wolf Tap to toss back a few with the old gang. It was that last shot Axl insisted they all do for old times sake that did it. Now he knew he'd had one too many. Not that he was drunk by any stretch of the imagination. He had a high tolerance. But his knowledge and experience told him he was probably in technical violation of the law.

Well just don't do anything stupid and get stopped, he told himself, sitting up straighter behind the wheel, gripping it in both hands and holding the pickup to the posted speed limit, a steady 50 miles-an-hour.

He glanced down briefly as he switched on the headlights. Starting up the hill, he clicked on the brights and swept into the curve and the sudden glare of a pair of headlights coming straight at him. Impulsively, he dug deeper for the inside of the curve, but the gravel shoulder was only three feet wide with a ditch cut extra deep to handle the rain runoff from the hill. As the truck hit the ditch it flipped over and rolled up the embankment, smashing the cab roof almost flat before wedging between two trees.

Miraculously, Jed walked away from the accident. Or rather, was driven away. By the State Police. To local headquarters. Where he registered exactly 0.10 on the breathelizer test. Because Jed was right on the line (if he had scored 1/100th less he could not have been charged with legal intoxication), the officer might have let him go with a warning citation, but because an accident was involved, "You could have been killed, or worse, killed somebody else," the officer felt Jed would benefit from a stern lesson and should suffer the discomfort and expense of going to trial, and thus charged him with DUI.

Jed would suffer all right. And not just the extreme inconvenience of trying to run his business without driving privileges for six months. By the time it was all over lawyers fees and court costs would run to $5,000 dollars. His auto insurance quadrupled - to $2,500 dollars a year, and his older, but meticulously well-kept pickup truck was a total loss. It was replaced by the insurance company with a broken down wreck, same model year, but worth only a fraction of what the truck he'd lost had been worth in terms of real utility. It would take Jed several years to pay off the debts incurred by the bank loans necessary to pay off his legal expenses, insurance, etc.

The next day the *Jefferson County News* ran a brief story on page two about Jed's arrest, noting yet another accident caused by a drunk driver. Thankfully, the story concluded, nobody had been killed. Not even the drunk that caused the accident. Fate had given him another chance, but should we? In a brief side-bar to the story, when the paper contacted Renee Cooley, President of MAIDS, for her comments, once again she reiterated her demands that even first time offenders should be given hard time when convicted of driving under the influence. As a deterrent to others.

After all, she went on, if someone had been killed in this most recent accident, wouldn't the drunk who caused it be, in fact, guilty of murder?

OTHER DREAMS

FOURTEEN

SAFETY FIRST

Feeling a little guilty for not stopping at the scene of the accident, Renee Cooley wheeled the car into the church parking lot and squealed to a stop in the first available space. Well, it wasn't *her* fault that the idiot had run off the road, she reminded herself. He was probably driving too fast for his old piece of junk truck and just lost control. She wasn't sure, but she could've sworn it was Jed Holiday's truck. Old fool was probably drunk.

Well, she didn't have time to worry about such nonsense. She threw the door open and swung out of the coupe. She had lives to save. It looked like everyone was already there, too. Waiting on her.

Oops. She hurried back to the car. She'd almost forgotten her purse - and her coffee.

But no one was waiting. In fact a vigorous debate was already underway. "You just got the Gray Wolf Tap's hours reduced to 1:00 AM only three months ago!" Hal Rankin, sometime PR man for the department, loudly exclaimed, "what more do you want?"

"They should be reduced to Midnight during the week and 1:00 AM on weekends," Anna O'Brien fired back just as loudly. "And we want the roadblocks increased to three randomly chosen nights during the week, as well," she added.

Rankin shook his head. "Look," he began in calmer tones, "if we force every business to close at midnight and set up floating roadblocks to check on who's out and what they're doing," he shrugged, "well, that would amount to imposing a curfew on adults."

"So what?" Every head turned to see Renee Cooley at the back of the room. She'd stopped just inside the door. Now that she had everyone's attention she went on. "Who needs to be out after midnight, anyway? Especially on week nights?"

"Yeah!" several women cried, among them Suzi Crisper, Rose Hillard, mother of Henry "The Weasel," and feisty 68-year-old Rachel Miller who owned Rachel's Cafe. "Safety first!" she chirped.

"Rachel's right!" Jeanette Bulger cried, "if we have to sacrifice a little freedom to make the community safer, then so be it!"

"I agree," Renee Cooley put in. "I mean, having freedom doesn't do you much good when you're dead. Just ask my daughter," she added somberly, "if she'll hear your prayers."

Rankin shook his head, took a deep breath, and started again. "I'm sorry about your daughter, Mrs. Cooley, but I don't at all agree with your philosophy. And what's more, I don't think the town council or the county will vote to once again further reduce the hours of drinking establishments."

A young Jefferson County officer had accompanied Rankin to the meeting and now he spoke up. "Besides, as a patrol officer, I personally don't want to sit the night at roadblocks. I and other officers I've talked to want to patrol. There's a lot of highway out there and a lot of back roads. A lot of homes and businesses to watch over. If we're all at roadblocks, not only do all the bad guys know exactly where we're at, and incidentally, there were 33 burglaries in this county last year, but so does everybody else, and they simply take routes that bring them around wherever we set up the roadblocks. In short, it's just not as effective as most people think, and if we're all tied up doing that, well," he shrugged, "we can't do much else."

Now Renee approached the front of the room and turned to the assemblage of women, mothers and housewives, the police officers, and Robert Renfrow, the 47-year-old elder minister of Saint Christian's Church and grade school. He was the only male who regularly attended the MAIDS meetings, more because of the fact that he didn't have much else to do than because it was held in his church basement.

"So then," she began, eyeing the veteran officer and his young protégé, "are we to conclude that the Jefferson County Police Department won't support us in either our efforts to further reduce the hours of drinking establishments or the increased use of roadblocks?"

Rankin nodded. "As PR man for the department, that's what I've been instructed to convey by my superiors, ma'am, and for the reasons given. It's a big county, and we simply don't have the manpower and funds to engage in these operations to the extent that your organization would like to see implemented, although the roadblock out on Route 32 on Friday and Saturday nights will remain in place indefinitely - at least at this point."

"Fine," Renee said frostily, "and you can tell that Sheriff of yours, Jim Nordic, that the MAIDS will certainly remember him come election time - but *not* with fondness, I can assure you."

OTHER DREAMS

FIFTEEN

BOUNCING BACK WITH BLACKJACK

Taterhead had to figure something out and he had to do it fast. Before he went stir crazy. Gaitlin at least still had his job to go to each day. For the time being, anyway. And while Tater had his hens to tend, that took up a very small part of his day and provided no income.

After feeding the hens, collecting the eggs, and mowing the grass, despair nipping at the edges of his heart, he went out back of the barn to collect crickets for fish bait in a jar with holes punched in the lid. Three crickets in the jar later he was thunder struck with an idea. Why not load up all his eggs, drive down to a big city like Rockford, find a likely spot to set up, and sell what he could off the back of his truck? Sort of like a little roadside stand? He'd seen people do it with lots of things before. Pumpkins. Watermelons. Sweet corn. Flowers. Any kind of vegetable you could name. And even shrimp and lobster on ice. Why couldn't he do it with eggs?

Excited, the fight back in him, he ran up to the house, set the jar of crickets on the back steps, went inside, found a big piece of cardboard and with a black Magic Marker made himself a sign announcing farm fresh eggs at $1.25 a carton.

They might've ruined him in Harlot, Taterhead thought to himself as he loaded up the eggs, but the world was bigger than

Harlot and damn it, his life *wasn't* over. He'd just figure out another way to do what he'd always done. Sell eggs. And if he sold them at a $1.25 a carton, his income would nearly double, what with his previous commercial price of .75 cents per carton.

Hah! He'd show the jerks. He'd come out *better* than before. A lot better. And he'd be sitting, too, and letting the customers come to him, rather than driving all over the county making deliveries. Think of the money he'd save in gasoline alone! And it was only 9:00 o'clock in the morning. He had the whole day.

45 minutes later Taterhead rolled into the outskirts north of town and spotted just what he was looking for. Or so he hoped. In the deserted asphalt parking lot of a boarded-up discount store, two black men, one rather elderly, the other rather huge, had battered pickups parked close to the road with big signs set up, one offering sweet corn, tomatoes and green peppers, the other watermelons.

Would they let him set up, too? Maybe they'd be racist about the whole thing or something. Taterhead didn't know. New to the game and a little nervous, he slowed and turned in.

Sitting side by side on their tailgates, both black men looked up and smiled as the old red Ford squeaked to a stop. "Hi," Taterhead said, offering a grin of his own.

"Yes sir, yes sir," the older, toothless one with the snow-white hair replied, dipping his head once on each "yes".

Taterhead paused, licked his lips and plunged right in. "Mind if I set up here next to you guys?"

The big one with the gold tooth and the watermelons shrugged. "What you sellin'?"

"Eggs."

"Shucks yes, young'un," the old timer with the white hair responded immediately, "you just go an' set up right here next to me, 'cause ifin' they stops to buy your eggs they might just buy some o' my corn, too!"

"Thanks," Taterhead said happily, the transmission slipping into gear with a *clunk* as he coaxed the old Ford into a spot beside his new friends.

Without wasting a moment he shut the engine down, jumped out of the truck, set up his cardboard sign and dropped the tailgate.

Now all they needed were customers. And they came. In a steady stream. All day long. But not before Taterhead had a chance to introduce himself.

"Hi, Randy Ellis," he said, extending his hand to the elderly gentleman that invited him to join them. "Just call me 'Tater', all my friends do."

"Tater," the old man repeated. "What that stand for?"

Taterhead went blank momentarily, then shrugged. "Heck, I don't know. Been so long I forgot."

"Ben," snow white offered a warm, dry, hand. "Ben Stone. An' this here Wally Winfrey," he motioned with his head at the man sitting on the other tailgate selling watermelons, adding with a chuckle, "an' he not related to Oprah, neither."

Taterhead laughed and took Wally's big hand, duly noting that it wasn't just the man's hand that was big, but his head, his torso, his arms. In fact the whole creature was massive. Funny, but he hadn't really noticed the extent of it when he first pulled up. Tater wondered why, but only for a moment, and then their first customer pulled up.

After the woman left with a carton of eggs, two dozen ears of corn and a watermelon, Ben Stone grinned a toothless grin and nodded at Taterhead, saying, "See Tater, ever thing gonna work out just fine!"

"Thanks, you guys," Taterhead said gratefully, looking at both men. "I really appreciate you lettin' me set up here."

"Shucks Tater, t'ain't nothin'. There be enough here for ever body," the old man said.

"Yeah, now if you was one a them Japanese," Wally put in.

"Yeah," old Ben interjected, "Damn Japs wreckin' the country, buyin' up all our stuff. Don't even gets me started!"

"Yeah," Taterhead sounded off with his own indignant if somewhat confused version of history. "If it hadn't been for us they would'a lost the war!"

At that both men chuckled delightedly, Wally Winfrey gesturing with a motion of his head, "C'mere."

Taterhead slipped off his tailgate and stopped between them. "What?" he asked curiously.

Leaning slightly to one side to expose the can of beer he had hidden just inside the truck, Wally asked secretively, "You drink beer, Tater?"

Sporting an easy grin, Taterhead nodded. "Yeah."

Pulling a cold one from a small cooler hidden in his watermelons, Wally said, "Here," and handed it to Tater. "But you gots to be discreet," he cautioned. "Don't let no customer or police drivin' by see you else they bust us."

"Yes sir," old Ben Stone put in, dipping his head once. "Them police come by a couple a times an' made us take the drunk test, but now they done give up."

"Yeah," Wally added. "Ya see, we don't set out here an' get drunk o' nothin' like that. We just likes to sip a little beer now an' then, but it be illegal outside."

"I know," Taterhead said, snapping the can open. "Thanks." With a quick glance around to make sure the coast was clear, he took a swig.

"Now you just hides that by your egg cartons an' when nobody here you can sip a little now an' then," Wally instructed.

"Thanks," Taterhead said again and returned to his own truck where he safely tucked the beer away just as another customer pulled up and got out of the car.

And so it went. Sippin' and sellin', the hours flying by, until all at once Taterhead was surprised to find he was actually enjoying himself. Heck, this wasn't working, he thought as he popped his fourth beer, this was partying and getting paid for it!

By 2:00 PM, the beer supply exhausted, Ben Stone, whose truck was in the middle between Taterhead's and Wally's, turned to the boy and said, "Your turn."

Taterhead blinked. "What?"

"We outta beer. Now it be your turn ta go get more."

"Oh. Okay."

"Liquor store just two blocks south," he pointed.

Taterhead nodded. "Sure, be right back." He slipped off the tailgate, went around to the cab, climbed in and started up the engine.

"Whoa, Tater!" old Ben called, "where you goin', young'un?"

Confused, Taterhead leaned out the window and looked back at the man. "To get beer."

The old man smiled and shook his head. Motioning with his fingers like a child waving goodbye, he said, "Shut 'er down, young'un."

Taterhead killed the engine, climbed out of the truck and ambled back. "What, Ben?"

"Just walk," Ben instructed. "It only be two blocks, an' that way you don't lose no sales whilst you gone."

"Oh. Is that the way you guys do it?"

"Sure," Wally Winfrey put in. "We always be watchin' each other's stuff."

After the past awful week Taterhead was grateful for this recent good fortune. It was almost too good to be true. And suddenly it occurred to him, maybe it *was*. Maybe they'd just drive off with his eggs and he'd never see them again.

Making friends can be a risky business. It means at some point leaving yourself vulnerable to, basically, a total stranger, thus allowing an opportunity for mutual trust and respect to grow. Eyes turned inward with this thought, when Taterhead refocused he noticed they were both watching him closely. Well, he'd just have to go with the flow and take his chances. Otherwise, a moment of suspicion and mistrust *now* might blow everything. "Okay," he said. "Makes sense to me."

"Sure it do," old Ben smiled and nodded once. "Don't you worry none, Tater, we look after your stuff just like it be our very own."

"Okay," Taterhead said again. "Back in a minute, then." He raised a hand in farewell and walked off for the liquor store two blocks south. He came back with a 12-pack which was divided between Wally's cooler and Ben's.

"So where you be from, Tater?" Ben asked as the three of them settled on his tailgate with fresh beers.

"Harlot."

"Ohhh," both men responded spontaneously and exchanged glances. Harlot was well known to the local black community as one of those white rural enclaves it was best to stay out of.

All of this, of course, was completely lost on Taterhead. He had no idea. Neither did most residents of Harlot. In fact it was only two young, ignorant-pig Deputy Sheriff's Police, Bill "Barnacle Bill" Barnickle and his best and equally corrupt friend, Ted "Dashing Ted" Dasher, responsible for Harlot's dark reputation with the black community.

With standard operating procedures like excessively long delays on simple ID checks during unwarranted traffic stops, busting young blacks on totally trumped up charges, and even two incidents of outright brutality which were simply brushed under the rug by authorities, their mission had been accomplished. No blacks would be moving to Harlot. Or even driving through.

"Harlot," Wally said somberly.

"Yeah," Taterhead swigged beer, adding innocently, "ever been there?"

"No." It was Wally.

Ben Stone coughed. It was time to change the subject. "Been around Rockford much?"

"Uh-uh," Tater shook his head. "My folks always said it was a dangerous place. Wouldn't let me come here when I was younger 'cause there were too many. . . " his voice fell off.

"Blacks?" Wally ventured a guess.

Glowing with embarrassment, Taterhead suddenly brightened with an appropriate answer. "Crime," he looked at them triumphantly.

"Well there sure be plenny a that," old Ben dipped his head once. "Yes siree, plenny a that. An' plenny o' poverty to go with it, too!"

"Yeah," Taterhead agreed a little sadly, kicking at a broken piece of asphalt with one sneakered toe. "The economy's really goin' down."

"An' the poorer ya are the harder you hits the pavement," Wally Winfrey put in.

"Ain't that the truth," Ben rejoined.

"Well thank God for chickens," Taterhead said on a lighter note.

"An' corn," old Ben piped up.

"An' hungry peoples," Wally Winfrey grinned. "Now who ready for 'nother beer?"

They all were.

The afternoon turned out to be as busy as the morning and by the end of it Taterhead only had four cartons left - and two pockets bulging with cash.

"Well give them ta me, Tater," Ben Stone said, gesturing at the four lone egg cartons on Taterhead's tailgate.

They were all packing up to leave in the golden light of early evening, the booming rush hour business having at last tapered off.

"Why?" Taterhead looked at him.

"'Cause I puts 'em with my grandson tomorrow an' then if he sell 'em, he keep a quarter for each one an' gives you a dollar. That be fair, don't it?"

"Sure," Taterhead said, lifting a shoulder, "but how's he gonna sell 'em?"

"I gots 'em set up on the south side a town doin' the same thing's us," the old man answered.

"Yeah, he be sellin' muh watermelons the same way," Wally Winfrey put in. "He get a quarter for them, too, ya see. Then we all makin' a little money an' nothin' left over ta go ta waste."

"Okay," Taterhead said, gathering up the four cartons and handing them over, "sounds like a good deal to me."

"That be right, young'un," Ben Stone smiled toothlessly. "Be a good deal for ever one. You just gets all the eggs out here you can an' we'll sells 'em on both sides a town."

"Great!" Taterhead exclaimed, adding, "what's your grandson's name?"

"Folks calls 'em 'Blackjack'. Must be right 'round your age, too." Setting the egg cartons in the back of his truck, when he turned around he said in surprise, "Well shoot, here he come now, Tater."

Taterhead turned to see a striking, spotlessly clean, white late model Ford pickup trimmed in flat black with smoked windows, brushed aluminum wheels and meaty tires. It rolled across the parking lot towards them with the deep-throated rumble of a strong V-8, and with a tiny squeak from one heavy-duty hydraulic shock absorber, came to a stop beside Taterhead and Ben Stone.

17-year-old Jack "Blackjack" Stone was so nicknamed by friends because once, unarmed, he'd taken down an older kid swinging a blackjack - and did it with a lightening quick swiftness that was still talked about in some circles. Looking at Taterhead now, he smiled. "Hi."

"Hi," Taterhead grinned back.

"What bring you this way?" his grandfather asked. It was unusual for Blackjack to come up to the north side after work. He usually just went straight home, which was south-centrally located.

Climbing out of the truck, he shrugged. "Don't know, got done early so I took a spin up here to see how you all were doin'."

"You sold *ever thing?*" It was Wally.

"Sure did," glancing Taterhead's way he added, "put someone new on the crew without tellin' me?"

Chuckling, his grandfather said, "This here Tater. Just started with us this mornin'."

"Tater," Blackjack repeated, extending his hand. "Blackjack."

They clasped hands tightly, each experiencing an immediate and inexplicable rapport as they gazed into one another's eyes.

When the moment passed each boy knew he'd found a new friend. "Got a beer, grandad?" Blackjack asked his grandfather.

"You outta them, too?" his grandfather grinned, pulling a beer from his cooler and handing it to him.

"Just finished my last one," Blackjack answered.

"An' that be my last one, too," his grandfather replied.

Blackjack lifted a shoulder. "No problem, me an' Tater'll just go get more." Turning to Tater, he gestured with his head, saying, "Come on, Tater, check out my ride."

With a glance Ben's way, Taterhead shrugged. "Okay."

"No, no," Ben Stone shook his head. "Me an' Wally here gots to be gettin' along, but ifin' y'all wants to go off an' have beer, well just go on along, then."

Everything was happening so fast Taterhead could barely keep up with what was going on.

"You want to, Tater?" Blackjack asked.

"What?"

"Get more beer? C'mon, I wanna show you my ride. Just got it two weeks ago."

"Lordy!" Wally grinned, shaking his head, "you an' that truck!"

"It look cool, don't it Tater?" Blackjack asked, watching him closely.

Taterhead nodded, "Yeah it does."

"So you wanna go?"

"Okay."

"You comin' back tomorrow, Tater?" old Ben asked.

"For sure," Taterhead answered. "What time?"

"Oh, not much happen before 9:00 or so 'cause it mostly be just folks hurryin' to work."

"Okay," Taterhead grinned and reached for the man's hand, "I'll be here with every egg I can lay my hands on."

Ben took his hand and smiled, "Sure enough, young'un."

Then the massive Wally Winfrey stood up, the pickup sighing with relief and rising several inches when he vacated the tailgate. "Good ta meet ya, Tater," he said as they shook hands, "see ya tomorrow, then."

"For sure." Turning to Blackjack, Taterhead said, "I'd better lock my truck up if we're gonna leave it settin' here awhile."

"Sure," Blackjack agreed. "Don't wanna leave your truck settin' 'round for just anybody to climb into."

At 5'7" Blackjack was only an inch taller than Tater, but lean and wiry with even white teeth and a ready smile, dark eyes set close and a finely chiseled nose with flared nostrils. Girls thought he was cute, and everyone knew he was faster than greased lightening - at anything he did.

"So what you think a my ride, Tater?" Blackjack asked as they motored easily down Route 51 heading south into town.

"Sure beats the heck out of mine," Taterhead grinned.

"Well you gots to get yourself a new one, my man," Blackjack returned the grin as he pulled into the liquor store parking lot.

"Ha! Wish I could," Taterhead laughed, "no money."

"Split a 12-pack?" Blackjack asked, turning to more immediate concerns.

Although he wasn't drunk, Taterhead *was* feeling the warm glow of having sipped beer all day, and considered that yet another 12-pack to share might be a bit much. Actually, what he really wanted was dinner. "You wanna eat first?" he asked, turning to his new friend.

Blackjack had more than a few beers thinning his own blood, and put a thumb and forefinger to his chin to consider. After a moment he looked at Tater and said, "Yeah, I could go with somethin' to eat too, I guess. What you want?"

As in any medium to large urban center in North America, there were more good things to eat in Rockford than Taterhead could even think about. "I don't know," he shrugged, "What'a you want?"

Blackjack raised his eyes to the ceiling for a thoughtful moment, then looked at Taterhead. "How 'bout Chinese?"

"Yeah!" Taterhead exclaimed, "I haven't had that since. . . since. . . I don't know when!" he finally concluded.

"Okay, I know the best place in town, but let's get the beer first and then we'll be all set. Here," he held out four dollars. "That should be about half."

Taking the money, Taterhead climbed out of the truck and went for the beer.

At The Three Chins, a little hole in the wall take-out place on the south side of town, they ordered shrimp chop suey, something Taterhead never had before, pork fried rice and egg rolls. Plastic forks and paper plates were provided compliments of the house.

They had their dinner at a picnic table in a city park nestled along the banks of the Rock River.

"You actually made a living *deliverin'* eggs?" Blackjack was dumbfounded.

"Well I didn't have any expenses," Taterhead countered, opening the fried rice carton. "In fact I still don't. I live with my folks."

Blackjack looked at him.   "That be a pretty good deal then, huh?"

Taterhead nodded. "Yeah. I'm able to save money."

"Like, between sellin' 'em on both sides a town, how many eggs can you supply?"

"Hmmm," Taterhead had to think about that one a moment. "I don't know," he shrugged. "Maybe as many as you can sell."

Looking interested, Blackjack passed him a paper plate. "You got any other products in mind?"

"I was thinking about getting a cow and learning how to make cheese."

Blackjack stopped what he was doing and looked at him. "I *love* cheese," he declared.

"And maybe I could learn how to make beer, too," Taterhead added.

"Beer?" Blackjack looked serious.

"Yeah."

After a moment Blackjack's face brightened and he said, "Well, *that* we'd have to sell under the table. They won't allow us to have no liquor license."

"No, of course not," Taterhead agreed. "But it'd probably be a good moneymaker."

"No doubt. Here, let's eat," Blackjack said, scooping steaming shrimp chop suey onto his plate.

"Your idea about under the table might just work," Taterhead said, tipping a carton and nudging fried rice onto his plate with a fork.

"No doubt," Blackjack said again. "Want a beer?"

"Sure." After they'd popped a few beers both boys hungrily dug in.

"Yeah, we gots us a little roving farmer's market here that do real good," Blackjack was saying between mouthfuls of fried rice. "Expanding the product line, that'd be good for all of us. What you can't sell on your own we'll sell for a .25 cent cut."

"Sounds good to me," Taterhead said, crunching into tasty shrimp and vegetables.

After dinner they took a walk along the river bank, their pockets stuffed with beers. When they got back to the truck they still had three apiece left.

It was well after dark by the time Blackjack got Taterhead back to his truck. They slapped hands, said their goodbyes, and then Taterhead got in his truck and drove home. And he was whistling all the way. He had to find a cow to buy. Research in the library on how to make cheese would take time, but that had to be done, too. At the same time he had to invest in his present business. More laying hens to buy. And now he'd have the money to do it.

OTHER DREAMS

SIXTEEN

HIGH NOON IN HARLOT

It was spray-painted in red on the underpass where the tracks went over Route 32 east of town: **Gaitlin,** then a big red heart with an arrow through it followed by **Taterhead,** and after that in parentheses, **(Town Faggots).**

Gaitlin saw it on his way home from work and he was pissed. He'd had enough. The bible says there is a time for war, and now as far as Gaitlin was concerned, it was. He was going to find out who put the graffiti up there and compel them to remove it. He didn't care who it was or how many were involved. And he didn't give a damn what it would take to compel them, either. Given the mood he was in, he felt he could do whatever it would take to get the job done.

He tossed around the idea of getting Taterhead involved but decided against it. He sure as hell could use the help and would welcome it, but Tater was going through enough what with the loss of his egg business and his impending court date on bogus sexual assault charges. And besides, the kid just wasn't a fighter. In fact looking back, Gaitlin couldn't remember Taterhead *ever* being in a fight during their entire school career going all the way back to grammar school. No. Leave Tater out of it. Gaitlin could handle it himself - or die trying. With the way he was feeling either outcome would suit him just fine.

Buzzing into town, he whipped the little Dodge Shadow around the corner, roared up Main Street and screeched into the first empty slot out front of the Gray Wolf Tap. Breathing fire and brimstone, he leapt out of the car, raced up the tavern steps, flung the door open and stormed inside.

There was a bright strobe-like blast of daylight as the door opened and banged shut behind him. Standing legs apart, just inside the door while his eyes adjusted to the dark, fists clenched and breathing heavily, Gaitlin loudly announced to anyone that didn't care to shut their ears, "Okay assholes, whoever put up the bullshit about me and Tater on the underpass east of town, front and center 'cause I'm gonna kick your ass up and down Main Street until you lick it off or paint over it or do whatever you want until it's gone!"

Every head in the place turned and stared, completely shocked to silence. Like a camera slowly coming into focus, Gaitlin was gradually able to see in the dimly lit room. A few local farmers and Dirk, of Dirk's Hardware, were scattered up and down the bar. Lowell Bordewith was behind it.

Shoving his glasses back on his nose, Gaitlin shifted his gaze to the row of red upholstered booths along the east wall and found what he was looking for. Axl, Bullets and Nervous were crowded into one side and staring openmouthed, the Weasel and Fat Bart, sitting opposite them, were twisted around in the booth and looking equally dumbfounded. No one had ever seen Gaitlin like this before. No one.

Nostrils flared and looking as wild-eyed as anyone they'd ever seen before, if anyone was going to tear up anybody, today it was going to be Gaitlin Tyler. "Bullets!" he roared when no one moved.

Dearly hoping Axl would intervene, Bullets muttered under his breath, "I'll kick his faggot ass. . . ." And then, much to his relief, Bullets felt Axl tense up beside him.

But just as Axl was about to make his move, Nervous Nate grabbed Bullets' arm and whispered harshly, "No! Blood! What if he's got AIDS and you punch him out and cut your hand on his tooth or his blood gets in your eye or something!"

Furious that Nate's interruption had, in the blink of an eye, put him squarely back in the ring at the exact moment that he was about to get out of it, Bullets roughly yanked his arm free, snarling, "Get off it, jerk!"

Surprised and hurt at Bullets' reaction, Nervous Nate whined, "I was just thinking of you."

"Yeah, right," Bullets said bitterly.

And it was then that his fear was becoming apparent to the others. They were shocked. They couldn't believe it. Bullets the invincible afraid of nerdy Gaitlin Tyler? The thought was unthinkable. But no. It was the AIDS. It had to be.

"Well Bullets, I'm waiting," Gaitlin said with deadly tranquility.

"Why me?" Bullets cried, pressing back in the booth with self-righteous indignation. "What makes you automatically think it was *me* who wrote that shit on the underpass?"

At that everyone turned and stared at Bullets. He'd just been bragging about it not five minutes before. Now he appeared to be running scared.

"Okay asshole," Gaitlin spat the words, "if *you* didn't do it, who did?"

Feeling every eye on him and almost glowing with embarrassment, Bullets protested in a voice that rose much too high and much too nervously. "How should I know?"

Unsure, Gaitlin's eyes moved to the rat-like mug of the Weasel, his orange hair, freckles, green eyes and prominent two front teeth almost glowing in the dimness. Next he took in Fat Bart, who looked pasty and pudgy like the Pillsbury Doughboy. Nervous Nate appeared to be his usual, anxious self, sitting up close on the edge of the bench seat and looking a bit lost by it all. Gaitlin already knew what Bullets looked like. Scared.

His gaze jumped to Axl, who looked confused. Suddenly it didn't matter how big he or his knife were. It was Axl's first encounter with a situation in which his power of brute force was utterly neutralized. By something he perceived as weakness. By something sickly. By AIDS. But he was really neutralized by his own stupidity and fear.

Gaitlin rested his gaze on Axl.

Startled at the brazen challenge, the big man flinched, one meaty paw instinctively sliding down for the big buck knife as he momentarily forgot that the last thing in the world he wanted was to cut this kid and get blood, *AIDS* blood, all over himself. But the heavy gray matter marbled with fat that was stuffed into his big round, crewcut head finally got the message through to the hand and Axl left the knife where it was.

Putting his hand on the table, Axl asked without the tough tone that was normally in his voice, "What, Gaitlin? What're ya lookin' at me for?"

"Because I want to know who put that shit up on the underpass, Axl. And I'll tell you something else, if you pull your big bad-ass knife on me," he shrugged, "that's okay, I'll just go get a bigger one."

"No," Axl immediately shook his head, eyes big and round in his big round face, "I'm not gonna do nothin' like that, Gaitlin, don't worry."

Gaitlin smiled thinly, saying pleasantly, "I'm *not* worried, Axl."

But Gaitlin was operating under a major delusion. He thought their discomfort and fear was due to his own fierce anger and a willingness to engage in physical combat. As though because he was angry enough to try and take them all on and was ready to, he somehow automatically became *capable*. And if this wasn't true how come they were all acting as if he could toss the lot of them through the front window like John Wayne in a movie?

At the moment it wasn't a dangerous delusion for Gaitlin - at least not until he started believing it himself. And then he did.

"Well I'm glad to hear you're not going to pull your knife, Axl," Gaitlin said, stepping further into the room. "But who's going to clean up the underpass?"

Axl stared at him, then shook his big crewcut head and replied as one falsely accused, "How should I know?"

"Because *you* know who did it, Axl."

Axl wasn't used to getting bullied, he was used to doing the bullying, and he didn't like this sudden reversal of roles. Especially by an AIDS infested faggot. In fact the whole situation was becoming patently ridiculous. Something had to be done.

Axl looked up and in his best "awe shucks" manner, timidly said, "It ain't true that I necessarily know who did it, Gaitlin, but I'm gonna try and do my best to find out for you, okay?"

Gaitlin pondered a moment, then cocked his head, asking like Clint Eastwood in a *Dirty Harry* movie, "When?"

"Oh, right now, Gaitlin, right this second. Just give me a chance to confer with the boys here, okay?"

"Yeah," Gaitlin nodded, speaking in soft, even tones, "I can wait a moment," he paused, "but don't be too long, sometimes even *I* get impatient." Then he turned, sauntered over to the bar and ordered a beer.

It was like *High Noon* in Harlot and Lowell Bordewith was anything but bored. In fact it was all he could do to keep from racing to the phone and calling everyone he knew to announce a showdown right in the middle of town - right in his place!

Axl glanced back once to make sure Gaitlin was out of earshot, then immediately turned his attention to the boys around the table and spoke in quick, hushed tones as their heads went together in a secretive huddle. "Okay, listen. All we gotta do is get 'em to attack us, ya know? But instead a fightin' back, we just back off an' keep on backin' off, 'cause no one wants to fight with him and maybe get the AIDS or somethin' beatin' the shit outta him, right?"

"No," Bullets quickly shook his head.

"Right. So we just keep backin' off until he starts goin' crazy an' stuff till finally we gotta hit 'em with a bar stool just to calm him down, right?"

Everyone in the close little circle nodded. They understood exactly what to do. They'd just turn the other cheek. Like Jesus. Until finally they'd have to subdue Gaitlin for his own safety - with a bar stool across his head or something. Everyone at the table slipped out of the booth and stood up, facing Gaitlin in a semicircle in the middle of the room, arms folded across their chests and looking very self-righteous.

After a moment Lowell Bordewith gestured towards them with a nod of his head and said to Gaitlin, "I think they're ready for you."

"Thanks, Lowell," Gaitlin said. Turning his back to the polished oak bar and leaning against it with his elbows, he took a swig of beer and inquired pleasantly, "Well, gentleman, have we come to a verdict?"

"Yeah, Gaitlin, we have," Axl spoke right up. "Nobody here knows anything about what's writ on the underpass, but if it's somethin' sayin' you an' Tater's a couple a corn-holdin' faggots, well," he grinned and gave a half-shake of his head, "we all believe it."

Suddenly Gaitlin's cool demeanor gave way to red-hot rage. As he blindly lunged at his grinning tormentors they quickly and easily parted, spinning Gaitlin off them and right into a booth. Catching the table edge at the hips, Gaitlin grunted with the pain as he slammed face-down across it, his eyeglasses skittering across the chipped formica and clattering to the dirty linoleum floor underneath.

This brought a burst of laughter from everyone, Bullets gleefully shouting, "What's wrong Gaitlin, get up on the wrong side of the bed this morning?"

Not bothering with his glasses and ignoring the sharp pain throbbing through his hips clear to the bone, in one motion Gaitlin rolled off the table and whirled around snarling, "I'm gonna kick your chicken-shit ass, Bullets!"

Moving aggressively towards Bullets, Gaitlin raised his fists, but just before he reached him, Nervous Nate quickly stuck a foot out and tripped him, causing Gaitlin to stumble into the bar stools, which brought another roar of laughter from the crowd.

Furious, Gaitlin whirled around, pointed at Nervous and shouted, "I'm gonna kick your ass too, Nate!"

"Ah ha-ha," Nervous Nate laughed, "you couldn't kick your way out of a brown paper bag, homo!"

"We'll see about that, moron!" Gaitlin bellowed, once again lunging at his tormentors, who were lined up like some kind of weird football team from someone's worst nightmare. He never had a chance. As he charged they all flowed around either side of him with the bait, Nervous, standing his ground. But long before Gaitlin reached him, Weasel suddenly spun around backwards, delivering a heel kick right into Gaitlin's groin.

Gagging, Gaitlin doubled over and hit the floor on his knees, at which point Axl gave Bullets the eye and pointed at a bar stool.

In an instant Bullets swept up the bar stool, arced it around in the air and slammed it across Gaitlin's head. And before anyone even realized it the whole thing was over.

OTHER DREAMS

SEVENTEEN

THE PLOT SICKENS

Hal Rankin stood grimly by while the medics removed Gaitlin on a stretcher, but there wasn't much he could do when everyone present said the same thing; Gaitlin Tyler went bonkers when he came in angry about the graffiti on the underpass, and started attacking everyone until somebody (in all the confusion nobody could remember exactly who) finally decked him with a bar stool. It was a sad state of affairs, sure, everyone agreed. But what could they do? Poor Gaitlin just went nuts.

After Rankin and the ambulance left with the still comatose young man, Axl cheerfully ordered up a round of drinks for the house and a party-like atmosphere quickly enveloped the growing crowd. Now, with Gaitlin out of the way (for nobody believed after such a beating that he would actually come back for more) it would just be a matter of time before they caught up with Taterhead and to Axl's way of thinking, evened the score for the sexual assault on his daughter.

Although the talk was of castration, almost everyone suspected what Axl really had in the works for Taterhead - sexual mutilation. A fine point, maybe, but in their sick, sadistic imaginations they wanted to see it happen. Or rather, witness Taterhead's reaction to his own murder. A murder that would be especially brutal because it would leave him alive. That was the interesting part. How would he react to the utter indignity of it? Suicide?

     *   *   *

Later that evening it was with a most perverse glee that Axl and his youthful companions, Kelsy "Bullets" O'Brien, Bartholomew "Fat Bart" Binks, Nathaniel "Nervous Nate" Naumann and Henry "The Weasel" Hillard drank their beer and plotted in Weasel's backyard.

Now that it was decided *what* Taterhead's punishment would be, the main problem the plotters faced, of course, was how to sever the lad's manhood from the main portion of his body without endangering themselves with his supposedly AIDS infected blood.

"It's really not going to be that much of a problem," Axl assured his young comrades-in-crime.

"Why not?" Bullets asked.

"Because," Axl shrugged, "first of all, I'm going to be doing the cutting. . . ."

"Yeah, but *we'll* be the ones doing the holding!" Bullets interrupted.

"No," Axl shook his head. "Look, all we gotta do is lure him out to Tess's Grove. . . ."

"Or drag him," Nervous Nate interjected.

"Or drag him," Axl gave a nod to Nervous. "And then tie him to a tree. After that I'll put on a full hood with face shield, rubber gloves, coveralls, the works. I do the surgery, cauterize the wound with a little propane torch so the kid don't bleed to death, and then we take him to the hospital, drop him outside the emergency entrance and scoot before anyone even knows we're there."

"But what if he's not?" Bullets looked at Axl.

"What?"

"Infected. Maybe he doesn't even have the AIDS. Seems like we're goin' to a lot of trouble for something he might not even have."

"Yeah, well why take chances?" Weasel countered, swigging beer. "What Axl's sayin' makes sense to me."

"Yeah," Fat Bart put in, "me too."

"All I'm sayin' is," Bullets began again, unwilling to drop the issue, "let's find out if he *does* have AIDS. If he don't then we don't have to worry about wearin' hoods and tying him to a tree and stuff. We could even do it right here in Weasel's backyard."

"No way," Weasel emphatically declined, "we're not doing it in *my* backyard."

Everyone pondered this in silence for some moments. At last Axl stood up to leave, saying, "To tell you the truth, I don't care if he has AIDS or not. I don't want *his* blood on me anyway. I say we stick with plan 'A'."

"Well who's going to lure him out to Tess's Grove?" Bullets asked, looking up at the man.

Axl drained his beer and set the empty on the picnic table. *"You,* Bullets," he said, grinning.

"Me?" Bullets looked shocked. "But I know he's. . . ." Bullets clapped his mouth shut just in time.

"What, Bullets?" Weasel asked. "You know he's what?"

"Yeah," Nervous Nate and Fat Bart both wanted to know.

Axl was looking pretty interested, too. "Maybe I should sit down and have another beer," he said.

Bullets was staring hard at him. If he spilled the beans now Erica. . . everything. . . would be blown. And he'd look like a total asshole. For one interminable moment Bullets teetered on the edge of saving his soul and damning himself forever. Choice. It was his. And nobody could take it away from him. Not even *God.*

"Ah, forget it," he said, waving them off and rising from the picnic table. "I'm getting another beer, anybody want one?"

OTHER DREAMS

EIGHTEEN

CONVERSATIONS WITH GOD

It was the rope. It made him nervous. Well they weren't going to *hang* him with it, for Christ's sake! Bullets berated himself. Parked in his father's pole barn, he popped the trunk lid, threw the rope in with the heavy rubber gloves, hood, goggles and coveralls Axl had given him earlier, looked around for the little propane torch, spotted it on the work bench, tossed it in the trunk as well and slammed the lid. Axl would bring the knife.

Still, it kept running through his mind like a recording he couldn't stop; *this is sick. . . this is sick. . . this is sick. . . .*

But over that, like a tape double-tracking, another, gentler voice breathed in his ear; *you can make up your own rules. . . which gives you an advantage. . . over the fools that follow the rules. . . .* It was almost like a song. A chant.

And then Pastor Renfrow's voice intruded; *you can always be forgiven. . . always forgiven. . . . Our father who art in heaven, hallowed be thy name. . . forgive us our trespasses. . . .*

"Stop!" Bullets shouted, pressing his hands to his ears. Startled at the sound of his own desperate voice echoing aloud in the dimness of the deserted pole barn, and suddenly afraid he might not be alone, he looked around.

But he was alone, and his pathetic cry for silence had worked - for the moment. And then the first voice started again; *this is sick. . . this is sick. . . .*

"Fuck it," Bullets muttered to himself, forcing the recording to the back of his mind. With great deliberateness he focused attention on his next problem. Namely, how to lure Taterhead out to Tess's Grove?

Well, he shrugged, slipping into his car, slamming the door and firing up the engine, it didn't matter. He had a few days to think about it. Or they could get lucky and just find Tater out there. Now that was a pleasant thought. Easy. Then, with this stuff already hidden out at the Grove they'd be all set to do what they had to do.

Had to do? His conscience questioned.

Yes, Bullets almost spoke aloud. Someone had to punish Tater.

For *what?* some part of his brain wanted to know. But was it some part of his brain? Or an *external* creature urgently trying to guide him away from making an eternally fatal decision?

For What? For attacking Erica, Bullets mentally responded. He had told this lie so often and so automatically that he actually started believing it himself.

Suddenly he felt sick like he wanted to throw-up. It had just occurred to him; for some strange and inexplicable reason he found himself in a situation where he was about to torture and maim Randy Ellis, a lifelong friend. Well, schoolmate, anyway. Why?

And he was walking through his part as one walking through a dream. But floating at the periphery of his conscience was a sick, desperate feeling that he was going to awaken out of this dream to find it was really a nightmare. *His* nightmare. So why do it?

Because Tater's a fucking faggot homosexual! Bullets silently exploded. Spreading AIDS. The bible says. . . .

You *know* your charge is false.

Well, well. . . fuck you, anyway! Bullets mentally stammered.

As ye judge so shall ye be judged. With the words of thine own mouth shalt thou be convicted.

Fuck you.

And then the recording started over again; *this is sick. . . this is sick. . . this is sick. . . .*

"This is fuck you," Bullets said aloud, looking at himself in the rear view mirror with a crooked grin. He was going to *enjoy* this, he snickered as his heart hardened to stone and the recording echoed away to nothing. Thank God! It was gone. Relief.

But for how long?

Bullets was too scared to even address the question. He put the car in gear and pulled out of the barn. He had to get down to Tyler's gas station before they closed. And lately it seemed they'd been closing earlier and earlier. In fact business had fallen off sharply immediately after word swept the community about Gaitlin's sexual orientation. And to make matters worse, his companion in perversity was the town lecher and mental basket case who had supposedly tried to lure three children into Tess's Grove for sex play - and then became enraged and attacked the children when they resisted his efforts.

No. The Tyler's wouldn't be living in Jefferson County very much longer. And they couldn't qualify for food stamps, it was whispered - too many assets.

Bullets was pleased to see the gas station still open at 4:00 o'clock. He rumbled up to the pumps and stopped in his gleaming blue Torino '72 with the shiny mag wheels and side pipes. Stabbing the accelerator once, he revved the engine and shut it down.

It was strange. Everything seemed so quiet in town. Like it was Sunday morning or something. Cocking his head, Bullets

peered into the station house. Where the heck was everybody?
As usual the door was propped open by the big yellow phone
book.

Bullets reached for the handle and was about to pop out of
the car when a work-gloved hand came to rest on the doorsill.
George Tyler, an eery flat tone to his voice, said softly from
behind, "That's okay. Stay in the car. What do you want?"

Once again Bullets felt a stab of fear. All of a sudden life
had turned upside down. Everything was different. He could
hear it in George Tyler's voice. He could *see* it in the gloved
hand on his door. "Gas," Bullets managed to squeak, his voice
so tight he thought he was going to choke.

"Gas," George Tyler said like a robot, his face a frozen
mask of passivity. Turning to the pump, he unfitted the delivery
nozzle, turned back, stood there holding it up and inquired
tonelessly, "How much gas?"

Bullets was stunned. My God! How'd George Tyler turn
into a Robot? It was getting like The Twilight Zone around here
he thought as he stared wide-eyed frightened at the man for what
must have been a long time. The passive expression remained
frozen on George Tyler's face, like he'd been lobotomized or
something. "I - I, fill it please," Bullets stammered, then hurried
to add with what sounded like a whimper to his own ears, "Mr.
Tyler."

But Mr. Tyler wasn't there anymore. He was at the back
of Bullets' car, fueling it with a look of tremendous concentration.

George Tyler was holding on. Tightly. He couldn't die
and leave Gaitlin this way - partially paralyzed and in the hospital.
Thank God he'd come out of the coma. George Tyler trembled
with emotion and raised brimming eyes heavenward with silent,
fervent thanks.

Bullets was sitting numb behind the wheel, holding it
lightly in two hands. The sinking feeling was starting to go away.
Fuck it, he finally told himself, just be glad *you're* not a robot like

him!   Startled, he jumped when he noticed the man standing beside his window.   It was as if he'd just materialized there.

Bullets forced himself to look at the man.   To lock eyes with him - and was shocked to discover he *couldn't!*   He absolutely could *not* engage the man's attention in any visual way!   "What?"   he managed to squeak through a tightly stricken throat.

"$15 dollars,"   George Tyler droned in his best robot voice, his face still a rigid mask of passivity.

"Oh, yes,"   Bullets found himself fumbling with his wallet.   He extracted a single $20 dollar bill and handed it to the man in the blue work shirt and coveralls.   "H-How's Gaitlin doing?"   he hurriedly managed to stammer before the man could get away.

"Gaitlin's in the hospital,"   George Tyler droned tonelessly with unseeing eyes.   Carefully slipping a five from the thin roll of bills he took from his pocket, he thrust his hand in the window and released the bill.   It fluttered into Bullets' lap.   When Bullets looked up again George Tyler was gone.

Boy, the world was sure getting weird, Bullets said to himself, tucking the fiver away and glad it sure as hell wasn't *him* that was getting weird.   He fired up the engine, revved it once and rumbled out of the gas station.   He had to get out to Tess's Grove, get this stuff stashed, and get back to the Gray Wolf Tap and let Axl know everything was set.   Everything except for how he was going to lure Taterhead out there.   Well, there was plenty of time for that.   By the way, where had Taterhead been lately?   He hadn't seen him around in days.

Relieved that, apparently, no one else was around, he parked in the shallow ditch along the road where everybody generally parked, loaded the torch, rope and other stuff into a giant, heavy duty green plastic garbage bag and slammed the trunk lid.   Not wanting anyone to see him heading into the grove with a giant garbage bag, which would require some kind of explanation he was unprepared for, Bullets glanced up and down the road to make sure the coast was clear, then hurriedly set off along the narrow trail that led into the stand of timber.

It was a gorgeous August afternoon buzzing with busy insect life, the sun high and hot, a gentle breeze carrying the scent of fresh mown hay. Traipsing along in the dappled sunlight and marveling at the beauty of the forest and the summer day that made it so, Bullets suddenly froze in his tracks. . . . Voices! He was almost to the circular clearing deep in the grove where everyone partied. He dropped to a crouch and listened closely.

They were speaking so softly he couldn't make out what they were saying, but he definitely recognized the voices. It was Kevin Crisper and Johnny Bulger. Bullets slowly stood up and peered into the clearing, but couldn't see anything. From the voices he could tell they must be sitting on the fallen log everyone used as a bench. Wondering just what they were up to, Bullets carefully hid the garbage bag in some trail-side foliage, then stealthily crept around the last curve in the trail. And there they were. Crouching behind a tangle of thorny brush, Bullets watched, a grin slowly spreading across his face.

As adolescent boys often will, Kevin Crisper and Johnny Bulger, their clothes scattered about the clearing, were sitting on the log innocently experimenting with the incredible sensations that mere touch could bring. They had no idea that it was a perfectly normal phase of sexual self-discovery that most boys go through. All they knew was that it was very bad, although no one had ever explained *why*.

Perhaps because no adult could. It was too shameful to talk about, and to do so in any positive way would be like endorsing immorality - like admitting that *they themselves* had engaged in such despicable, perverse behavior.

With sudden, re-awakened memories of himself and the Weasel experimenting in much the same way only 10 years before, Bullets watched in silent fascination as Kevin Crisper gently and

"Yeah," Bullets grunted heavily.

"W-what's gonna blow us away, Bullets?" Kevin stammered with a trace of nervousness that he hoped no one noticed. Resenting the intrusion, he wished Bullets hadn't shown up at all. Besides, he had no interest in Bullets and his big hairy, gross-looking cock. He only liked jackin' with Johnny. But what could he do? They'd been caught and now he had to go along or else Bullets might broadcast it all over town about how he'd caught Kevin and Johnny wackin' their wangers in the woods. And then his father would probably find out, Kevin realized with a sudden jolt of fear. And what with the way he carried on about Taterhead Ellis and homos and fags, Kevin was sure his dad would probably take out the gun and shoot him.

All these heavy thoughts had wilted Kevin's erection completely. Oh well. He was sick of this game anyway, and certainly wasn't looking forward to whatever it was Bullets had in mind. But he felt trapped. Heaving a weary sigh, he realized he'd just have to stick it out. Even death would be better than his father, let alone the whole town, finding out that he and Johnny were a couple of wienie wackers.

As for Bullets, he had finally reached the pinnacle of his depravity. Not because he was engaging in sexual activity with these two adolescent boys, which at best constituted criminal sexual abuse of a minor, and at worst, psychologically speaking, was something akin to rape, but because of the gross hypocrisy his life had become.

And Bullets was loving it.

OTHER DREAMS

NINETEEN

AN ACADEMY AWARD PERFORMANCE

Taterhead got up earlier than usual, quickly did the chores, fed the chickens, and started collecting his load of eggs for the day. When everything was ready, the eggs boxed and on the truck, he went back to the house, made himself a bowl of cereal and sat down to eat and peruse *The Farm Journal* for ideas. Maybe it was time to invest in a couple of champion setting hens and more rapidly increase his supply of chickens, which would more quickly increase egg production.

Flipping through the magazine and slurping milk and corn flakes, he heard the floor boards above creak as his mother slowly made her way downstairs. "Morning, ma," he said, glancing up as she shuffled into the kitchen looking especially haggard and beat, as if the night's sleep hadn't refreshed her at all.

Mumbling "Morning, Randy," she made her way to the stove and clattered about with her old coffee pot, lit the ancient gas appliance with a stick match and set the pot on the burner to percolate. With a tired sigh she sank down at the table opposite him and stared dully for a moment before asking with no real curiosity, "Where're you off to so early?"

"Got eggs to sell, ma," he said, tossing the spoon into the empty bowl with a clatter.

"You got your route back?" she asked in surprise.

Shoving his chair back, he got up and went to the sink. "No," he said over his shoulder as he rinsed the bowl and spoon and placed them in the drainer, "I'm doing it a new way."

"Oh?" His mother sounded interested.

"Yeah," he turned around and leaned against the counter. "Down in Rockford. Me an' some other guys got a little roadside stand set up. I'm sellin' 'em right off the back a my truck and making more money than ever!" he grinned, adding, "I'm not beat yet, ma."

His mother smiled weakly at this good news. His sheer enthusiasm said far more than his words ever could. "Good for you, Randy," she nodded, "you just keep that attitude, son, and you'll do all right."

"I will," he assured her. "Don't worry, 'cause things are gonna get better - I promise."

"All right, Randy," she smiled again, a little color actually coming into her face.

"Well, gotta get going," he said, suddenly shoving off the counter and heading for the door. He wanted to get to Rockford early so he'd have time to hit the south side where Blackjack was set up. The day before, Blackjack had sold all four cartons Ben had taken. This morning Taterhead was going to leave Blackjack with eight to see what would happen.

*   *   *

Bullets got up early, too. 1:00 PM to be exact. And after his afternoon of wild sex with the kids and a hard night of partying with the boys, he was feeling pretty wiped out. Bloated and bleary-eyed and sore in places he hadn't been in a long time, he didn't know why but it seemed he just hadn't slept well the night before. He didn't realize it then, of course, but he'd probably never sleep well again.

It was only 2:30 in the afternoon and by sheer coincidence Bullets, Fat Bart, and Axl all showed up at the Gray Wolf Tap at the same time - early.

"I don't know," Bullets shrugged as they slipped into a booth. "I haven't seen Taterhead around in days." He looked at his two companions. "Has anyone?" he frowned.

"Afternoon, Lowell," they all exchanged greetings as the already inebriated proprietor brought a round of beers.

Axl had gotten off work early due to finishing up a project ahead of schedule. Another plumbing job wouldn't be starting until Tuesday, but he didn't mind. He was looking forward to the long weekend. "Maybe he left town," the big construction tradesman suggested and took a long, gulping swig of the first beer of the day. In 10 minutes he'd be calling for another.

"Nah. Not without Gaitlin," Bullets remarked with a knowing smile.

Axl and Fat Bart snickered at that, Axl wondering aloud, "Well where the heck's he been?"

The three of them looked up when the door squeaked open and slammed shut with a bright burst of daylight and Weasel hurried to their booth. "Guess what?" he said, slipping in beside Bullets, "I just saw Taterhead."

"Where?" everyone asked at once.

"In Rockford," Weasel grinned, "sellin' eggs off the back of his truck at a roadside stand."

"Okay, here's the plan," Axl said at once, the four of them huddling close as the big plumber spoke in hushed whispers.

           *   *   *

"Well, first I'm gonna buy a couple a champion settin' hens," Taterhead explained as he, Wally, and Ben sat on Ben's tailgate sipping beer. "I already got four lined up, and they're in their egg laying prime, too."

It was just after 3:00 and the afternoon rush was beginning to build. For the next three hours or so they'd be doing more selling than sipping and they were getting their last ones in.

"Here come a customer," Ben announced as all three automatically moved to stash their beers.

Looking up, Taterhead instantly recognized the shiny blue Torino with the mag wheels and uttered an impulsive "Uh-oh."

Both black men looked at him curiously. "What, Tater?" Ben asked.

"Nothin', nothin," Tater quickly said as the Torino pulled up and stopped.

Keeping his eye on Taterhead, Bullets reached for the switch and killed the engine, the accustomed smirk that lately seemed to be on every familiar face from town curiously absent. By way of greeting he made an upward gesture of his head.

Taking a deep breath, Taterhead approached the car and stopped at the window. "What, Bullets?"

Looking serious and drawn, Bullets worked his lower lip a moment before saying apologetically, "I just want you to know everybody feels real bad about what happened to Gaitlin."

"Gaitlin?" Taterhead's voice rose with concern.

"Yeah," Bullets said, frowning. "You didn't hear what happened to him?"

"No," Taterhead replied with a shake of his head.

"He's in the hospital."

"The hospital?"

Bullets was genuinely surprised. He couldn't believe Taterhead didn't know. . . . "Since day before yesterday."

Sensing a presence, Taterhead caught a peripheral glimpse of Wally standing at his shoulder watching and listening carefully. "What happened?" Taterhead asked, turning his complete attention back to Bullets.

Apparently mystified, Bullets lifted a shoulder and shook his head. "No one knows," he admitted after a silent moment.

"Everyone says he just came stormin' into the Gray Wolf all freaked out and started attacking people until someone decked him with a bar stool. Anyway, I'm surprised you don't know about it," he added. "Everyone's been worried about you, wonderin' where you've been and all."

"Really?" That anyone in Harlot would be worried about *him* was in itself surprising to Taterhead.

"Yeah, everyone feels real bad about Gaitlin, too," Bullets went on, "seein' him hurt like that. And not just about that but about everything that's been going on over the last week. Everything just got out of hand, Tater. I think we all went a little crazy or something. Even Axl's not mad anymore. Thinks maybe Erica *was* stretching the truth a little."

"He does?"

Staring down at the dash, Bullets nodded vacantly, then turned to Taterhead. "Everyone wants you to come back. Start over. Forget the whole thing."

"Really?" Taterhead asked, hope springing anew in his pounding heart. Everything was going to be all right after all!

Bullets nodded again. "Yeah, and we're gonna have a little party out at Tess's Grove tonight - take up a little collection for Gaitlin just to let him know we're all behind him." He paused. "Everyone's hopin' you'll come, Tater. We. . . we were hopin' you'd be the one to take the money to him in the hospital, what with you bein' his best friend and all." Looking despondent and sorry as hell, he asked in a small voice, "Will you?"

Holding Bullets with a long, steady gaze, Taterhead licked his lips in thoughtful apprehension. "All right," he answered after a moment, "I guess so."

Bullets nodded appreciatively. "Thanks, Tater. Everything's gonna be different now. You'll see."

"Okay, Bullets," Taterhead said, "thanks for coming by to let me know. I'll be there."

"Great, Tater," Bullets said conclusively, extending his hand. They shook on it. "See you tonight then," he said, reaching for the ignition. The starter motor whined briefly. The big V-8 popped once and rumbled to life.

"I'll be there," Taterhead said again, raising a hand in farewell. "Bye."

It had been a fine performance. Definitely worthy of an academy award, Bullets thought to himself as he gave a final wave and roared off. Heck, maybe he should head out to Hollywood.

"What all that about?" Wally asked as soon as Bullets was gone.

Staring after the shiny blue car quickly accelerating up the highway, Taterhead turned back to Wally with an introspective grin and replied absently, "Nothin', Wally, nothin'."

Taterhead wasn't the least bit interested in getting his old route back - on that score his future was settled. But it would be nice to at least be friends with his friends again and not have to worry about being attacked or having his truck vandalized. And now with Axl's new attitude - and Erica's, surely he wouldn't have any serious legal problems when court came up next week. Sure.

With the afternoon gone and evening pressing in, Blackjack showed up just as his three business associates were packing up. "Here, Tater," he said, climbing out of his meticulously kept white pickup and handing him eight dollars.

"You sold all eight cartons?" Taterhead asked, not really surprised.

"Well that's not a charity donation," Blackjack grinned, adding, "could'a sold eight more if I'd had 'em."

Tucking the money into his jeans, Taterhead nodded. "You will, Blackjack, just give me a little time to build up stock." And then an idea occurred to him. "Want to go to a party?"

At that both Wally and old Ben looked up with concern, Wally catching Blackjack's eye and slowly shaking his head.

Momentarily distracted, Blackjack shifted his gaze back to Taterhead. "Uh, what sort'a party?"

But before Taterhead could answer, Ben and Wally came over, Wally cautioning, "That not a good idea, Tater. An' if you wants *my* two cents, you best stays away from that boy you was callin' 'Bullets'."

"Why?" Taterhead looked at him in surprise.

"'Cause that boy, somethin' ain't right with that one, Tater. He no good. I can just tell."

"You listen to Wally, Tater," old Ben put in. "Wally gots a way a tellin' about peoples. He think that boy got some evil hangin' around 'em, Tater."

"He from Harlot, too," Wally added, catching Blackjack's eye.

"That where you want to go party, Tater? In Harlot?"

Taterhead nodded, "Yeah." Then added curiously, "What's this thing you guys got about Harlot, anyway?"

All three black men exchanged glances before Blackjack gave a half-shake of his head. Perceiving Taterhead's naivete on the matter he explained with the hint of a smile, "Harlot don't like black folks, Tater. It ain't no place for us to go."

Taken completely by surprise, Taterhead queried in a rising voice, "Harlot?"

All three nodded, Blackjack adding, "It ain't no place for us, Tater."

Looking at them with a measure of perplexity, Taterhead said, "I never heard of that."

"You serious?" It was Blackjack.

"Yeah," Taterhead answered at once. "I wouldn't say people in Harlot are perfect or anything, but they're not *that* bad. I never heard of anyone being against blacks or anything like that."

"No?" Blackjack squinted at him.

Tater shook his head. "No way. Besides, you'll be with me. I wouldn't let nothing happen to you."

His curiosity piqued and having complete trust in Taterhead, Blackjack shrugged. "Well, what kind of party you be talkin' about?"

"Well. . . " Taterhead paused, "sort of a coming home party for me an' my best friend, I guess."

"Comin' home party?" Wally looked at him. "You been away?"

Looking uncomfortable and certainly not wanting to go into detail, Taterhead shrugged again. "Sort'a."

"What you mean, sort'a?" Ben asked, watching him closely.

Taterhead hemmed and hawed for some moments, shuffling around before finally admitting, "Well, there was some trouble before. Some kids were stealin' my eggs and I caught 'em and there was a big fight and everyone got mad at me but I didn't do nothin'. I guess now we're makin' up. They want me to come to this party and take the money they're collecting to my friend in the hospital. I just thought it'd be cool if Blackjack met some of my friends, is all. I mean, 'cause we're gonna be goin' into business together and stuff."

Blackjack looked at his grandfather and Wally for some moments, then said, "Why not? I want Tater to meet some a my friends one a these days too, so why should I be afraid to meet his?"

"Yeah," Tater put in. "If I was to go with you and meet your friends you wouldn't let anything happen to me, right?"

"No way," Blackjack answered immediately.

"So, the same goes for me."

"Okay," Blackjack bobbed his head once, "I'll go."

"And on the way we can stop and visit my best friend in the hospital."

"Sure, that sound like a plan."

"I don't know, Blackjack," Wally looked doubtful.

"Well Tater here's okay, ain't he?" Blackjack answered. "So I'd expect his friends be okay, too."

Old Ben shook his head, his face deep lines of concern. "I don't mean no offense to Tater, but I just don't think it a good idea for you ta be goin' up to Harlot." With a defiant nod of his head he added, "An' that all I gots to say on the matter."

"Ah," Blackjack waved him off. "I never been up to Harlot." Then he added with a snicker, "I ain't afraid a no ghost!"

Everyone had a chuckle over that except Wally, who retorted gravely, "It ain't no ghost we be talkin' about, Blackjack, an' if you goin' up to Harlot I'm goin' with ya an' we gonna follow Tater in your truck."

"That be a good idea, Wally," old Ben put in. "You go up there with the boy. that be a real good idea."

"Well sure that's a good idea," Taterhead quickly put in. "Why not? Wally can meet my friends, too."

Blackjack heaved a sigh. "Okay. I guess so if that's the way you want it, grandad." He was disappointed only because he'd wanted to ride with Taterhead, although the idea of bringing his own truck along *did* sound like a good idea - just in case.

"Great!" Taterhead grinned. "Let's go. We'll stop at the hospital on the way."

OTHER DREAMS

TWENTY

DAZED AND CONFUSED

Thinking a visit from friends would be just the thing for the injured young man's sagging spirits, when Taterhead and his companions presented themselves to the nursing station the head nurse immediately called for an aide to show the three of them to Gaitlin's room.

Taterhead was shocked. He hadn't known what to expect of course, but Gaitlin was in far worse shape than he could have imagined. There were needles in his hand, tubes up his nose, one eye was swollen shut and his whole face was black-and-blue.

With the nurse's aide standing by to make sure they were indeed benevolent visitors, Taterhead approached the bed. When Gaitlin opened his one good eye and offered a trembling, lopsided smile, Taterhead couldn't help exclaiming, "My God, Gaitlin! What happened?"

Doped up on painkillers, Gaitlin had been fading in and out of consciousness all day. Obviously dazed, he said thickly, "I guesh I jush losh it, Tater."

Staring in wide-eyed disbelief, Taterhead asked with tightly controlled emotion, "Who did this to you, Gaitlin? Tell me. I'm goin' to the cops."

Again Gaitlin managed a weak, lopsided smile and shook his head slightly. "Nobody knows," he whispered hoarsely.

"Nobody knows?" Taterhead looked at him quizzically.

Slightly moving his head from side to side, Gaitlin's one good eye slowly closed.

"I think that's enough questions for awhile," the nurse's aide gently intervened, "we don't want to upset him."

"No, of course not," Taterhead looked at her briefly. "I just want to tell him one more thing."

The nurse's aide gave a single nod of assent.

Moving around to the other side of the bed, Taterhead took Gaitlin's one good hand, the one without needles stuck in it. "Good news, Gaitlin," he said softly.

Gaitlin's eye opened.

"It's all over. This whole mess. Everybody feels real bad about what happened - everything. They're having a party tonight and they're gonna take up a collection for you and from now on everything's gonna be just fine, okay? Understand? This whole nightmare is over."

Floating through a fog of drug induced confusion, Gaitlin offered another trembling, lopsided smile and nodded slightly. "Thanksh for comin', Tater," he whispered thickly, "an' wash out for. . . wash out for. . . ." Damn! Who the hell *was* Tater supposed to watch out for? Half his face grimacing with frustration, the other half paralyzed, Gaitlin spluttered and frowned with the effort to marshall his thoughts.

"I think that's enough for now, Mr. Ellis," the nurse's aide intervened. "The most important thing Mr. Tyler needs is rest, not distress."

Tightlipped, Taterhead nodded. Looking down at Gaitlin once again, he said softly, "Bye, Gaitlin, I'll come by tomorrow. You'll be feeling better by then."

"Wash. . . wash out. . . ." At last heaving a tired sigh, he muttered, "Tater."

"It's time to go, Mr. Ellis," the nurse's aide interjected.

"Yes, ma'am," Taterhead said, letting her draw him to the door. Wally and Blackjack, leaning against the back wall, pushed off and followed.

Returning down the corridor the way they had come, Taterhead turned to her and asked, "How come only half his face smiles?"

"He's experiencing a slight paralysis on his right side," she answered. "Nerve damage. But the doctor expects full recovery over time," she hastened to add.

Taterhead stared at her. "Thank God for *that,*" he sighed.

Pushing through the double plate glass doors for the parking lot, Taterhead turned to Blackjack and Wally and said, "Shucks, I wanted to introduce you to him, but I don't think he even knew you were there."

"That be all right, Tater," Wally said as they headed for their trucks, "we'll meet 'em another time."

"Sure we will," Blackjack put in, adding, "but I think he tryin' to warn you 'bout somethin' an' just couldn't get it out, Tater."

Tater shook his head. "Nah. He don't really know about the latest developments, Blackjack. He don't know it's all over."

Blackjack stopped and took Tater's arm. "Maybe 'cause it ain't," he said evenly.

After a thoughtful moment Tater shook his head again. "Nah. It's over."

Of course part of the reason Bullets had been so believable that afternoon was because Taterhead *wanted* to believe him, wanted the whole thing to be over, forgotten, and relegated to the distant past as quickly as possible.

"Okay," Blackjack shrugged, "you be the one to know better than me."

But Taterhead didn't know. Taterhead was hoping.

OTHER DREAMS

TWENTY-ONE

THE PARTY FROM HELL

The sun was a giant red ball sinking behind the cornfields, and the locusts were noisily grinding away in the trees when Blackjack tooted his horn and pulled up beside Taterhead's truck on the county blacktop just north of town. As both trucks slowed to a stop he leaned forward to see around Wally and shouted, "Hey man, if we be goin' to a party shouldn't we be bringin' some beer?"

"Nah," Tater replied, "they'll already have beer there. And I'm the guest of honor," he added with a bright smile.

"Okay, my man, it's your show," Blackjack grinned, "we be followin' you, bro."

Taterhead nodded. "It's only about a mile up the road."

"I don't like this one bit," Wally said worriedly as Tater pulled ahead and they fell in behind.

"Well hell, Wally, I what'n born yesterday neither. I ain't just gonna go waltzin' in to no woods in this here white boy country. I figure, you know, we hang back first, see how things look. If they cool we go in, if they ain't cool we skedaddle outta there right quick. Say?"

"Uh-huh," Wally nodded, "we might just lives longer that way, too."

"Yo', bro!" Blackjack grinned and held up his hand. They slapped five and then Blackjack said, "Uh-oh, here we are."

Up ahead they saw Tater's brake lights glow brightly as he pulled to the side and parked in the shallow ditch behind four other vehicles. "Don't look like that big a party to me," Wally commented in a huff.

"Everybody probably rode together what could fit in four cars," Blackjack shrugged.

Wally was doubtful. "I just don't like the smell o' things 'round here, Blackjack. That boy that come an invite Tater this afternoon, there be somethin' evil hangin' 'bout him. I'm tellin' ya."

"Ah," Blackjack waved him off, "you just gettin' superstitious in yo' old age."

"You dang right I'm superstitious," he said with a sharp nod of his head. "You believe in God?"

"Course I do."

"That be superstitious."

"So?" Blackjack looked at him.

"So if there be a God there be a devil too, an' I thinks we gonna see one tonight. An' he ain't no Indian, meanin' *red,* he gonna be *white* this time!"

With a chuckle and a shake of his head Blackjack popped the door open and swung out of the truck. "Come on, Wally. Like I said, we be hangin' back just to make sure."

"Well, okay," Wally said, climbing out of the truck, "but I still don't like it. Not one bit."

Taterhead was looking slightly perplexed when they walked up. "Not as many people here as I thought there'd be," he said, quickly adding, "oh well, more people'll probably show up later. It's still early yet."

The sun was gone now, the blue sky streaked with purple, the horizon glowing with the rich red color of fresh blood as the three of them, Taterhead leading, set off single file down the trail that twisted and turned through the forest.

"Listen, Tater," Blackjack began as they trooped along. "At first me and Wally gonna hang back some."

"Hang back?" Tater spoke over his shoulder.

"Shhh!" Blackjack whispered harshly. "We don't want anyone to know we even here just yet."

"I don't get it," Taterhead said with a compliant whisper.

"It be like this, man," Blackjack continued patiently as they followed the winding path amidst the gathering gloom, "we both plenty nervous 'bout bein' here to begin with, and then all this strange stuff you talkin' 'bout at the hospital with your friend an' ever thing. Well, it makes sense for us to hide out first an' make sure your friends be as cool as you think they is. Then, if we find they ain't we can just skedaddle an' no harm be done to no one."

Taterhead nodded, continuing at a steady pace as he said over his shoulder, "Oh. Okay. But you really don't have to worry, Blackjack, these guys are basically okay. I known 'em all my life."

"How far up this place be?" Blackjack asked, suddenly a bit nervous himself about going to Taterhead's party.

"Just a little further," Taterhead answered, feeling a little funny himself about all the whispering.

In the darkness of the grove ahead was the faint orange glow of a fire reflected in the upper branches of the trees - and voices. Blackjack and Wally froze in their tracks, Blackjack quickly grabbing Tater's shirttail for fear he'd walk right into the circle of revelers still talking over his shoulder.

"Okay," Blackjack whispered harshly, "now you understan', right?"

Taterhead nodded dumbly.

"We just gonna hang out here for awhile, make sure ever thing cool, an' when we see it is we come an' party witch ya'll. But don't say nothin' 'bout us till we come, okay?" he cautioned.

Somewhat perplexed, Taterhead nodded.   "Well sure, guys, you don't gotta worry nothin' about me."

"I know we don't, Tater - someday you'll understan'."

"Okay," is all Taterhead could think to say. "Bye." And then he turned and continued up the trail with only a single glance back. But Blackjack and Wally were already gone.

"Let's don't get too close, now,"   Wally whispered nervously as he and Blackjack stealthily crept through the thick of the forest, around underbrush and over and under fallen trees leaning at crazy angles.

Leading the way, Blackjack shook his head. "Uh-uh, just close enough to see an' hear what's goin' on."

At the perimeter of the circular clearing, just beyond the reach of the firelight, they settled behind a tangled thicket and laid on their stomachs where they had a clear shot of the whole scene.

Taterhead was already there, having stopped just beyond the mouth of the trail. "Hey, guys," he was saying with just a hint of nervousness. "Where is everybody?"

The five of them, Axl Erickson, Kelsy   "Bullets" O'Brien, Nathaniel   "Nervous Nate" Naumann, Henry   "The Weasel" Hillard, and Bartholomew   "Fat Bart" Binks were all standing around a big, crackling fire swigging beer and looking at Taterhead in a way that struck Wally as oddly self-conscious. Blackjack picked up on it too.

"We *are* everybody," Bullets said, offering the infectious grin that had served him so well all his life. Flipping the cooler lid up, he pulled a bottle out, popped the top and flicked the cap into the fire. "Welcome back, buddy, come on over and have a beer," he said, extending the bottle towards Taterhead.

Doing the famous Taterhead shuffle, the slightly perplexed boy, a rather trusting soul imbued with a certain simple-minded honesty, ambled over and took the beer Bullets held out for him. "Thanks."

Almost beside himself with joy over how smoothly the task assigned him had gone, Bullets gave him a slap on the shoulder and said cheerily, "Don't mention it, buddy."

Again Wally and Blackjack were struck with the oddly self-conscious way the other's eyes silently followed Taterhead's every move. Almost hooded and serpentine in some strange, inexplicable way. And suddenly Blackjack was gripped with the startling fear that Wally had been right. There really *were* white devils! And he was lying on the ground in the dark of the forest only a stones throw away watching them.

Taterhead was feeling it, too. Or at least he was feeling *something*. But he didn't know what it was. Having never been touched by evil, he didn't recognize evil even as he stood in the midst of it. Maybe it was just the heavy, warm air of August pressing in. Maybe it was just his own dark imaginings and fears haunting him. Dismissing it all, he decided to drown his misgivings in beer and took a long, healthy chug, wiped his mouth with the back of his hand and innocently asked, "So, how'd the collection for Gaitlin go? You get a big one?"

"Oh yeah, real big," Weasel grinned. "Look," he pointed to a bulging green plastic garbage bag sitting by the huge old oak that graced the circular clearing 10 feet from the fire pit.

Feeling vaguely sick inside, Taterhead blinked and turned his gaze on Bullets.

"Well go on, Tater, take a look. We got a lot a stuff for Gaitlin."

Taterhead walked over to the garbage bag feeling as though he were floating through a dream, parted the green plastic folds, peered inside, and pulled out a heavy coil of rope. Bewildered, he held it up. "What's this?" he blinked.

"Here, I'll show you," Bullets answered pleasantly. Motioning with his head for the Weasel to follow, he crossed the clearing in five wide strides.

"You stand here," Bullets instructed, taking the coil of rope as he gently backed Taterhead against the tree. Handing the coil off to Weasel but hanging on to one end as the other boy started around the trunk, he added gently as if coaxing a child engaged in a difficult task, "That's it, arms at your side." Taking a step back as Weasel came around the other side, they made a knot securely binding Taterhead to the massive trunk. "See?" Bullets smiled warmly.

"No," Taterhead's voice trembled, "what're we doing this for, Bullets?" And he tried smiling, too, just the way everyone else was - except for Weasel, who seemed oblivious to it all as he continued diligently coiling the rope around the tree and the boy who was now bound to it.

Only after Bullets and Weasel deftly tied off the second knot and Taterhead was clearly held fast did Axl leave his place by the fire and approach the tree. As Fat Bart and Nervous Nate quickly joined him there, both sporting leering grins on their strangely contorted faces, Axl inquired in a lilting tone, "Remember what I said I was gonna do to you for attacking my daughter?"

"No. . . " Taterhead whimpered.

"Really?" Axl smiled, slipping the big buck knife out of its leather sheath.

"But I didn't, Mr. Erickson," Taterhead sniffled, suddenly trembling so hard the guys could've sworn they heard the leaves of the tree rattling.

Or was it the bushes at the perimeter? Bullets turned to look but didn't see anything and quickly turned back to watch the show. He didn't want to miss a single thing.

Axl turned the blade up and without warning, leaned forward, put the tip in the zipper and in one motion flicked Taterhead's jeans open. "Pull 'em down, Weasel," he ordered.

Weasel sprang to it.

"Underwear, too."

"Heyyy," Bullets grinned, "you're pretty well hung, Tater!"

Taterhead's breath was coming quick now, sweat running down his face as he cajoled, "Come on, guys, this ain't funny."

"Wanna play with it one last time, Tater?" Axl chuckled.

At that everyone burst out laughing.

"Go on, Tater, you can reach it. Might as well. For old time's sake," Axl grinned, "'cause this'll be the last time you ever get to play with it again."

But by now hot tears were spilling down Taterhead's cheeks. Racked with heart wrenching sobs, he could no longer hear above his own protestations of innocence - which were really nothing more than the guttural grunts of a human spirit realizing it was about to endure a humiliating fate worse than death. And it would last a lifetime.

OTHER DREAMS

TWENTY-TWO

WHERE ANGELS FEAR TO TREAD

The blood was pounding in Blackjack's ears so hard he couldn't hear his feet hitting the ground, only feel the jarring thump every time they struck the hard packed dirt trail. And he wasn't going to sacrifice an ounce of speed to chance a look back, either. And my God, Wally! He'd never seen such a big man run so fast in his entire life. He was already clear out of sight around the next bend!

At the trail head Blackjack skidded out onto the road and with sneakers slapping the pavement, took off for his beloved black-trimmed white pickup and got there so fast he couldn't slow down in time, thumped off the side and landed on his ass in the middle of the road. "What you doin', Wally, what you doin!!?" he screeched, leaping to his feet.

Wally was already sitting in the truck, staring straight ahead and gasping for breath. Turning with eyes bugged out big as golf balls, he bellowed maniacally, "What I doin'!? I's gettin' the hell outta here, that what I doin! They gonna cut that boy's wienie off!"

Sucking wind himself, head down between his arms as he leaned against the driver's door with both hands, Blackjack adamantly shook his head. "We can't," he gasped, "leave Tater like this!"

"You crazy, boy!" Wally screeched. "If they gonna do that to a *white* boy, what you think they gonna do ta you an' me!?"

"Can't leave 'em, Wally," Blackjack rasped, struggling for breath. "Couldn't face God as a man if I did."

"You crazy, Blackjack! What we gonna do against five white boys? No, we just run up the road here an' call 911. That what we do!"

"Be too late by then an' you damn well know it, Wally," Blackjack said, at last able to breathe again. Shoving off the door, he went around to the back and pulled out a four-foot crow bar, adding with determination, "I'm goin' back there an' bustin' up *that* party even if I has ta do it myself!"

Coming around the other side, he stopped at Wally's window. "You comin' or not?" he asked angrily.

Slowly shaking his head, Wally said, "Lordy, Lordy, yo' grandad never forgive me ifin' I let you go back there alone."

"Good. Grab the claw hammer an' let's go!"

10 seconds later both men were sprinting along the road and down the trail into the misty dark gloom of the forest. And they were so quiet and so fast no one saw or heard them coming.

The boys were standing around their victim laughing and jeering while Tater, his head hanging, quietly wept for his manhood. Axl, off to one side and caught with the heavy hood and face-mask half on, never had a chance.

Shrieking like a couple of crazed banshees, they stormed the clearing, Blackjack targeting the big one in the hood first. Taking a two-fisted grip, he swung with every ounce of strength he could muster, the crow bar humming as it *whooshed* through the air and thudded off Axl's chest, snapping three ribs and his left arm like toothpicks as he skidded ass-backwards in the dirt.

And when the startled youngsters looked up and saw the giant black man high stepping it across the clearing at hair raising speed, bellowing insanely and coming straight at *them* with the claw side of the hammer raised, they scattered so fast into the inky blackness surrounding the fire-illuminated clearing that it was as if a black hole had sucked them in.

Seconds later all that could be heard was the frantic snapping and cracking of four terrified boys crashing headlong through the underbrush. When Wally turned around the only sign of Axl that remained were a pair of heavy rubber gloves, a hood, and a face-mask scattered across the clearing to the mouth of the trail.

Overwhelmed with relief, Taterhead was laughing and crying all at the same time as Blackjack pried his bonds slack with the crow bar and held them aloft. Ducking under and out, Taterhead pulled up his pants. "You guys saved my life!" he cried and threw his arms around Blackjack, hugging him tightly like a man drowning.

"Now calm down, Tater, just calm down," Blackjack said, gently disengaging himself from the boy's tight embrace and heaving a sigh of his own as the hot adrenaline pounding through his veins gradually receded.

"Guess we won't be seein' anymore a them tonight!" Wally allowed himself a nervous chuckle.

"Wait!" Blackjack interjected, holding up a hand for silence.

A moment later there was the roar of engines being frantically started, the screech of burning rubber against asphalt and the rapidly accelerating whine of four vehicles straining against the night, their panicked drivers desperately trying to flee a monster they would never be able to elude - themselves.

OTHER DREAMS

TWENTY-THREE

TO SERVE AND PROTECT

Taterhead was crying. With relief. With profound sadness. When Wally had volunteered to drive his truck, encouraging the distraught boy to ride with Blackjack, Taterhead gratefully accepted.

Now, as they drove south of Harlot on the county blacktop, Wally leading the way back to Rockford and avoiding the highway out of fear of roadblocks, Blackjack was afraid Tater was losing it. Trying to calm the boy down, he said gently, "Now don't you worry none, Tater, you comin' home with us an' ain't nobody gonna try an' hurt you there."

"I - I know," Taterhead stammered through his sniffles. Wiping at his nose with his sleeve, he hiccupped and said, "It's just that I can't believe what's happening to me. One day my life's perfectly normal an' the next it's turned upside down." All at once his breath started coming in little staccato bursts as tears spilled anew. "An'. . . an' that they'd actually do that to me. I mean, they used to be my *friends!*"

"Friends like that ain't no good, anyway, Tater," Blackjack assured him, suddenly startled to see headlights looming large in his mirror. "I Wonder what be this dude's problem?" he said as the car, instead of passing, quickly slowed and began tailgating. And then he noticed the light-rack and muttered, "Uh-oh."

County Mounties Bill "Barnacle Bill" Barnickle and Ted "Dashing Ted" Dasher agreed on most everything, and especially on keeping niggers out of Harlot.

"Hey," Barnacle Bill said as he rapidly slowed behind the striking black-trimmed white pickup, "do I see a white boy up there riding with a burr-head?"

"That you do, that you do," Dashing Ted grinned.

They were both coming down from a pretty decent high, having shared a reefer two hours earlier while shooting radar up on Route 32. No tickets. No busts. Wasn't much traffic, everybody that didn't have to be out sticking pretty close to home these days. Too scared. You could get busted for sitting too long at a stop sign.

"Let's pull 'em over and check this out."

"You got the wheel, buddy, it's your call," Dashing grinned again. He always grinned when he was high. That's why they called him "Dashing".

Unknowingly, when Barnacle Bill turned on the strobe lights he turned off Taterhead's sprinklers.

Watching in his mirror as Blackjack was pulled over, Wally wisely kept going. After all, there wasn't a damn thing he could do about it - and stopping just wasn't the thing to do if you were black and in the vicinity of Harlot.

"Well, gentlemen," Barnacle Bill began amiably as he strolled up to Blackjack's window, "we in a bit of a hurry this evening?" His partner had come around the other side and was now keeping a close eye on the passenger.

"I wasn't speeding," Blackjack frowned.

"I'll be the judge of that," Barnacle Bill snapped. "Got a driver's license?"

"Sure do," Blackjack replied, reaching for his wallet.

"Got some ID, son?" Dashing Ted asked Taterhead.

"Yeah," Taterhead said with a tired sigh.

"Well you look like hell, boy," Dashing Ted said as Taterhead handed over his driver's license. "You boys been drinking tonight?"

"Heh-heh," Blackjack couldn't help letting a little chuckle escape before answering for Taterhead, "No sir, haven't had time. Been too busy savin' my friend here from gettin' mutilated."

"What's that?" Dashing Ted looked up from where he was closely examining Taterhead's driver's license with his flashlight.

Burning with humiliation, Taterhead said tightly, "Some guys tried cutting off my. . . ." The words stuck in his throat.

"Dick?" Dashing Ted commented absently and returned to examining the license. "Hmmm, Randy Ellis," he said half to himself, then looked up. "Now why would anyone want to do that to *you?*" Looking at his partner through the cab, he repeated, "Randy Ellis. Now where have I heard that name before?"

Barnacle Bill looked up from examining Blackjack's license and caught his partner's eye. "Kind'a rings a bell, don't it?"

"Yeah." Brows furrowed in thought, Dashing Ted suddenly brightened. "Yeah, right. This is the guy tried doing that 13-year-old girl in the middle of Main Street last week. I remember the State's Attorney talking about it when we were in court. Remember?"

"Yeah, right. That's it," Barnacle Bill said.

"Like children, huh Randy?" Dashing Ted grinned at the boy and winked.

Glowering, all Taterhead could do was sink lower between his shoulder blades.

"Well if you attacked my daughter I might try and cut your dick off, too," Dashing added.

With an expression of utter disbelief Blackjack looked from one officer to the other and back again, exclaiming, "The guy tried cutting the dude's cock off an' you not gonna do nothin' about it?"

The two Jefferson County sheriff's deputies exchange amused looks, Barnacle Bill inquiring quite seriously, "And what would you have us do about it, son? I can't arrest a man for *trying* to commit a crime, I gotta catch him actually *doing* it."

"Yeah," Dashing Ted put in. "If that were the case, you could get mad at your friend here tomorrow and come to us and say he *tried* robbing you. We can't arrest him for *trying,* we gotta get him with the goods. He's actually gotta *do* the crime before we can arrest him."

"Yeah," Barnacle Bill couldn't help stifling an amused chuckle, "so if we catch this guy with your cock in his pocket we'll nail 'em, okay?"

Raising his shoulders, Dashing said, "I mean, come on, what'a ya want from us?"

"Yeah, well there be such a thing as *attempted* murder," Blackjack said with offended indignation, "what about that?"

"It's a hard thing to prove," Barnacle Bill said matter-of-factly, "and besides, when's the last time you heard of someone being charged with *attempted* sexual mutilation?"

Dumbfounded, both boys just stared at the man. It was true. But then, how many reports of castration or sexual mutilation were there in Jefferson County? Neither boy thought to ask. The answer would have been none.

"What about attempted rape?" Taterhead suddenly looked up. "You hear about *that.*"

"Ahhh, that's one of *your* specialties, eh Randy?" Dashing Ted grinned.

"Wait," Barnacle Bill held up a hand. "It's a legitimate question. Let me answer him." He paused, catching Taterhead's eye. "The simple answer is that attempted rape's a hard one to prove, too. You gotta have some physical evidence of the attempt. Bruises, cuts, injuries of some type, witnesses.

Something. You can't just say 'somebody tried to rape me', and presto, we go out and arrest the person."

"Yeah, well what about this thing they callin' date rape?" Blackjack looked at the man.

Exchanging a knowing glance with his partner, Barnacle Bill shrugged and handed Blackjack his license back, admitting, "Hey, on that one you got me. It's something new. I don't even understand it myself. What can I say?" They had decided to let them off easy.

"My advice to you, Randy," Dashing Ted said, giving Taterhead his license back, "is to stay clear of this guy that's after you, 'cause until he hacks off your pee-pee there ain't a whole helluva lot we can do."

Chuckling, both officers sauntered back to their patrol car. In spite of everything they still had a soft spot in their hearts for the downtrodden and dispossessed. At least, that is, when they were both catching a good buzz.

OTHER DREAMS

TWENTY-FOUR

ONWARD CHRISTIAN SOLDIERS

There is something about the change of seasons in Northern Illinois. One day it's August and summer, and then with the flip of a calendar it's September - and autumn.

Maybe it's the disappearance of kids from the streets and lumbering yellow school buses everywhere. Or vast, empty stretches of highway suddenly devoid of RV's and cars towing motorboats. Deserted city parks and state campgrounds. Back-to-school specials advertised on TV and children in new clothes toting books and pencils and notebooks. All at once, though, the days seem shorter, the wind from out of the west cooler, and everyone knows the frosty nip and gray, cloudy days of November are just around the corner.

Whatever it is that makes September September, Gaitlin knew the moment he gimped through the hospital door with his cane - summer was over. He paused and took a deep breath of the sweet fresh air, grateful at last to be free of the antiseptic smell and oppressively warm, stringent, atmosphere of the hospital.

"How's it feel to be out?" his father asked, releasing the door he held aside for his son and the boy's mother.

"Great!" Gaitlin grinned, craning his neck back to look at the blue sky, his lungs swelling with another huge breath of sweet sunshine and air. "Thought I was gonna die in there!"

"Oh now, it wasn't that bad, Gaitlin, was it?" His mother smiled.

"I don't know, ma. 10 days in the hospital felt like 10 years to me."

The doctors were pleased and surprised at Gaitlin's rapid recovery. The slight paralysis of his deadened right side, and thus the need for the cane, would pass too, they were sure. The damaged nerves that carried muscle control messages from the brain just needed time to heal. In fact there had already been significant progress, which in itself was proof positive that full recovery was almost inevitable.

Would the tremors in his right hand go away, too?

Uh, not sure. Only time would tell about that.

What about the shaking, then? If it didn't go away could he learn to control the shaking in his hand?

They weren't sure about that, either. But he had certainly responded well in the physical therapy sessions, the doctors assured him.

These were bitter thoughts and Gaitlin pushed them away as his father and mother joined him on the sidewalk, his father saying with a stab at cheerfulness, "Well it's certainly a beautiful day!"

"Yeah," Gaitlin sighed, "let's go." Still not used to walking with a cane, he slowly and awkwardly hobbled out to the parking lot and his father's car.

"We have some good news for you," his mother said with a knowing smile as they got in the car, "but we wanted to wait until we got outside to tell you."

"Oh, what's that?"

"Taterhead was exonerated by the judge in court today."

"Well, not *exonerated,*" George Tyler corrected his wife. "But all he got was probation."

Gaitlin looked at his dad and smiled. "See?"

"Yeah, yeah," his father said and started the car.

"How long's he on probation for?"

"Five years," Marybell Tyler answered.

"Five years!" Gaitlin exclaimed. "Wow. That's a long time for something he didn't do."

"Yes, it is," his father admitted with a tired sigh, not wanting to get into one of *those* discussions again and fighting down a sudden bitterness that came welling up from deep inside. But it wasn't Gaitlin's fault, he had to continually remind himself, although at the same time he wasn't quite sure just who *was* at fault. For everything. For the virtual loss of his business, his standing in the community, his small social circle of friends. The loss of his whole way of life.

They were going to have to move. But How? He didn't have any substantial savings. They'd been running even for years, just barely making it. Thank God Gaitlin had hospitalization through the company he worked for. Or used to. If it hadn't been for that, well, George Tyler didn't know what.

"Where's Tater now?" Gaitlin was surprised he hadn't come by with the good news himself. After all, he'd been in to visit Gaitlin at least every couple of days over the last 10.

"Oh, I don't know," his mother answered vaguely. "No one sees him around much anymore ever since. . . ."

"Hasn't been by the station in two weeks," George Tyler quickly interrupted his wife. "Hear tell he's practically moved down to Rockford."

"Yeah, he told me he made some new friends out that way and was spending a lot of time there."

No one, including Taterhead himself, had breathed a word to Gaitlin about the mutilation attempt. Naturally his parents didn't want to unduly upset their son while he was in the hospital.

As for Taterhead, it was simply too humiliating to talk about. But even more so, it was just such an unthinkable and grotesque thing that they, and Taterhead too, had simply blotted it from their minds - at least on any conscious level. In short, they dealt with it by pretending it hadn't happened. Out of sight, out of mind, out of reality. Case closed.

But it wasn't. As far as the community-at-large was concerned Taterhead got off scot-free. And they were outraged. Once again the legal system had failed to deliver justice, or so popular opinion had it, and the residents of Harlot were fed up. Thus, when word got around about Axl's plans for Taterhead, there was scarcely a single dissenting voice - and that was the subject of Pastor Robert Renfrow's sermon on Sunday.

"Friends, neighbors," he began when the congregation had settled and the coughs and rattling of church bulletins had ceased, "I've spoken with many in the community during the last week and share your disappointment in the outcome of Tater. . . er, Randy Ellis' trial in the sexual assault of 13-year-old Erica Erickson."

He paused, cleared his throat and continued. "In fact, disappointment is probably an understatement of your feelings regarding this matter. Nevertheless, it's clear that once again the justice system has failed to deliver justice. The question then remains; need we subject ourselves to the determination of a corrupt judicial system which has strayed so far from the purposes of God? I think not, for although we are bound by the civil laws of this country, ultimately we are under the law of God - and for us *that* is the highest law."

Sniffling, he opened his bible to the first of several previously marked places and said, "I now read from Romans, beginning at chapter one, verse 24: Wherefore God also gave them up to uncleanness through the lusts of their own hearts, to dishonor their own bodies between themselves: Who changed the truth of God into a lie, and worshipped and served the creature more than the Creator. For this cause God gave them up unto vile affections: for even their women did change the natural use into that which is against nature. . . ."

The Tyler's had never been big church-goers. For them it was a Christmas and Easter thing, and that was about the extent of it. But Gaitlin, feeling abandoned, lonely, and depressed, had awakened Sunday morning, dressed, and decided he might find some solace in church. To do some good old-fashioned soul-searching and seek relief from his bitterness through prayer. After all, if he couldn't find God in church, where *could* he find Him?

He arrived 10 minutes late, the big double doors of the church standing open to a gorgeous September morning. Struggling up the broad stone steps, taking them one at a time, leaning on his cane and heaving his deadened right leg up each one, he gained the landing just as Pastor Renfrow started verse 27 of the chapter he was reading.

It stopped Gaitlin cold. Instead of going in and taking a pew at the back as planned, he slipped unnoticed into the foyer and off to the side, sank to the floor and sat with his back to the wall to listen.

"And likewise, also, the men," Pastor Renfrow continued reading, "leaving the natural use of the woman, burned in their lust one toward another: men with men working that which is unseemly, who," (he skipped to verse 32) "knowing the judgment of God, that they which commit such things," (and here he got loud) "ARE WORTHY OF DEATH, not only do the same, but have pleasure in them that do them."

With a dry little cough Pastor Renfrow flipped to another previously marked page and continued reading from Jude chapter one, verse eight: "Likewise also these filthy dreamers defile the flesh, despise dominion, and speak evil of dignities." Skipping to verse 14, he continued reading, "But Enoch also, the seventh from Adam, prophesied of these, saying, Behold, the Lord cometh with 10 thousand of his saints, to execute judgment upon all, and to convince all that are ungodly among them of all their ungodly deeds which they have ungodly committed." (Here he skipped to verse 16) "These are murmurers, complainers, walking after their own lusts. . . ."

The good Pastor quickly flipped to the next previously marked passage, second Peter chapter two, verse 12 and continued; "But these, as natural brute beasts," (he got loud here) "MADE TO BE TAKEN AND DESTROYED, speak evil of the things that they understand not; and shall utterly perish in their own corruption." (Here he skipped to verse 22) "But it is happened unto them according to the true proverb, the dog is turned to his own vomit again; and the sow that was washed to wallowing in the mire."

Looking up from the Good Book, Pastor Renfrow said, "Ladies and gentlemen, the law of the land says we must tolerate homosexuals in our community who turn to their own bodily secretions for pleasure, as a dog turning to its vomit, and that we must allow young men to roam the streets, the lusts of their bodies running rampant until, out of control, they attack our children. But the law of God demands that we do *not!* And ultimately if we, as Christians, forego the law of God in favor of the law of the land, then how can we call ourselves Christians? How can we call ourselves the children of God?

"In Conclusion, let me read to you from Timothy Chapter one, Verses 19 and 20, about two young men the apostle Paul put to death. And keep in mind, these young men were *not* caught engaging in homosexual acts, and they had *not* attempted the rape of a child." He paused dramatically, scanning the congregation. "Then what *was* their crime?" he continued. "Merely this: As members of the one and only church of God that existed at the time, they spoke against certain teachings that the Apostle Paul, through divine inspiration, judged to be blasphemous. I read to you from Timothy; Holding faith, and a good conscience; which some having put away concerning faith have made shipwreck, of whom is Hymenaeus and Alexander," (here he got loud again) "WHOM I HAVE DELIVERED UNTO SATAN, that they may learn not to blaspheme."

Raising his eyes to the hushed congregation, Pastor Renfrow said, "Gentlemen, ladies, the message, I think, is clear. The Apostle Paul, inspired of God, in his own turn served as executioner to rid the church of filth." Pausing to take a breath, he continued. "In our society we have a system of justice to mete out punishment, but when that system breaks down, when it fails to function, what choice are we left with?

"Let us not forget, that while some of us lead relatively simple lives, going to jobs each day and trying to raise our children, others among us are down in the trenches, battling the evil close at hand. And if the father of a sexually assaulted child watches his child's assailant arrogantly walk out of a court room scot-free, well, all I can say is, maybe it *is* time this young man was made an example of - and I think you know what I'm talking about. Maybe that's why he was born. To serve as a stern warning to child molesters and the perverse among us who prefer turning to their own vomit. And in conclusion, all I can say is, thank God there are men among us willing to take on certain tasks which the rest of us tremble at and shrink away from! And perhaps," he added as an afterthought, "when all is said and done the authorities will be as lenient on Axl Erickson as they were on his daughter's assailant."

Pastor Robert Renfrow closed the Good Book, said simply, "Go in peace," and apparently distraught, retired to chambers beyond the podium at the back of the church.

As the organist struck up the first notes of the closing hymnal and the congregation rose and began to sing, Gaitlin struggled to his feet, pushed his glasses back on his nose and with grim determination, gimped down the steps and around the side of the building for the rear. He was going to have a talk with Pastor Robert Renfrow.

With surprising quickness and dragging his dead leg after him, he climbed the three concrete steps of the little porch and banged on the back door with a fist.

The door opened almost immediately, the Pastor, his jacket removed, tie loosened and shirt collar and cuffs open, was sweating profusely and looking not a little uncomfortable at this surprise visit. "G-Gaitlin," he stammered.

"I'd like to have a word with you."

"Why, yes, of course," the good Pastor replied, stepping outside and letting the door close behind him. "My, it sure feels good out here!" he exclaimed, straining at exuberance.

"Yes, and it's not even a sin," Gaitlin replied, locking eyes with the man.

After a moment the minister cleared his throat and said with what he hoped was a tone of authority, "Yes, well what can I do for you?"

Unsure just where to begin, Gaitlin simply said, "Pastor, I heard your sermon from the foyer. You're inciting those people against Taterhead."

"And you," Pastor Renfrow fixed him with a hard stare, thinking, *okay kid, you wanna play hardball?*

Gaitlin's mouth was working, but no words were coming out. He couldn't quite believe it. "H-How?" he stammered. "Why?"

"I believe my sermon made that perfectly clear, Gaitlin," he replied curtly. "You know, the bible tells us that homosexuals should be put to death."

Staring in utter disbelief, Gaitlin could only think to say, "I don't know about the bible. . . ."

"You wouldn't," the minister retorted.

"Look, sir," Gaitlin began, getting a grip on himself, "What if Tater's innocent?"

"Of engaging in homosexual activities with you or assaulting Erica Erickson?"

"Both!" Gaitlin hotly replied.

"Well, you know the biblical rules. . . ."

"No, I don't," Gaitlin cut him off.

"Two or more witnesses is sufficient for conviction. So far *three* witnesses have testified as to your homosexual activities with Taterhead, and practically the whole town saw Tater tear the clothes off that poor child's back right in the middle of Main Street!"

Robert Renfrow looked down at the boy gravely. "What, exactly, is it that you want from me, Gaitlin? Do you expect me to condone your own and Tater's perverse behavior?" he asked with knitted brow. *"That* I cannot and will not do."

After a moment he continued in a gentler tone, "But if you'll renounce your relationship with Tater, confess your offense, and ask the Lord Jesus to come into your heart, I will welcome your return to the congregation."

All at once Gaitlin was speechless. His first inclination was to simply punch the man, but with a trembling right hand pressed to a cane supporting a partially paralyzed right leg, that wouldn't work out too well even if he *had* dared to be so bold. Gaitlin stared at him for one long moment. Finally, in quiet, dry tones he said, "I don't behave perversely." He couldn't help adding, "Asshole."

Pastor Robert Renfrow smiled tightly and said with quiet conviction, "You're going to burn in hell, Gaitlin," and then he turned and went back inside.

It was no longer just a case of Bullets losing his soul. The whole town was. For once they imagined their actions to be just retribution before God for Taterhead's perceived sexual assault on a child, compounded by his engaging in homosexual activities with Gaitlin, what *couldn't* they do to these boys that wouldn't be justified before God? After all, according to their understanding of the bible, God advocated *death* as the penalty for Taterhead's and Gaitlin's crime. All they were going to do was mutilate the

one boy for attacking a child. And aside from the beating Gaitlin
had already received, they were letting him off the hook entirely.
How merciful.

OTHER DREAMS

TWENTY-FIVE

STAYING HUNGRY

It was unusual to break down and clean a weapon *before* using it, but it hadn't been fired in so long Gaitlin wanted to make sure it was in absolutely perfect working order. Thus were all the parts to the army semiautomatic .45 caliber pistol laid out on the table in the screened-in porch that overlooked the backyard. Carefully cleaning each part with a little brush, oiling it and setting it aside on a spread out newspaper, he had to pause occasionally until the spasmodic trembling in his right hand subsided.

"Gaitlin?" His mother was standing in the kitchen door that let out onto the screened porch. She sounded worried.

"Yeah?" Gaitlin answered as he continued working.

"What're you doing?"

"Cleaning the gun, ma, what's it look like?"

She was silent for some moments before asking, "But why?"

"'Cause I figured it needed a cleaning. It hasn't been done in a long time."

"Oh. Well dinner'll be ready at 6:00. I'm making your favorite - roast beef with mashed potatoes and gravy with buttered peas and a salad."

"That's okay, ma," he said, continuing to work with intense concentration, "I'm not hungry."

Again there was a long pause. "Well, it's only 4:00 o'clock. Maybe you will be by 6:00."

"I don't think so, ma."

At 6:00 o'clock he intended on being out behind the barn at the Ellis place. He just wanted to practice-fire the weapon left-handed. He was sure Mrs. Ellis would let him if he asked.

OTHER DREAMS

TWENTY-SIX

FIVE FOR HELL

"We're never going to be able to lure him out to Tess's Grove again," Axl said, his left arm in a cast supported by a sling around his neck. He was in Weasel's backyard, one foot on the picnic table bench, his right arm resting on his knee as he spoke with Bullets, Weasel, Nervous Nate and Fat Bart.

"Well what do you suggest?" Bullets asked, taking a swig of beer.

"Grab 'em."

"Grab him?" Bullets looked at the man.

"Yeah," Axl nodded like it was the stupidest question in the world. "Every morning he goes home to feed the chickens and collect his eggs. All ya gotta do is wait till he gets south a town on his way back to Rockford, run 'em off the road in Weasel's old bomber and grab 'em. Then drive 'em out to Schlockrod's pond down by the tracks where I'll be waitin' for ya."

"When?" It was Weasel.

"First thing tomorrow morning," Axl said, draining his beer and setting the bottle on the table with a *thunk*.

OTHER DREAMS

TWENTY-SEVEN

LUCK OUT

The evening before when Gaitlin had gone to the Ellis' to practice-fire the weapon, he asked Mrs. Ellis about Taterhead and where he was staying in Rockford. Mrs. Ellis confessed that she didn't even know. Taterhead hadn't told her out of fear that in her absent-mindedness she might tell the wrong person. But Mrs. Ellis did tell Gaitlin she was certain if he came by at 6:00 the following morning he could catch Tater feeding the chickens and collecting his eggs.

Now it was 7:00 AM. Gaitlin had overslept. Hurriedly dressing, he thought if he raced over there he might still catch him. Pulling on his work boots and slipping into his denim jacket, he snugged the big .45 into an inside pocket and went out to his car.

Pulling into the Ellis' driveway he knew immediately that Tater had left already. But just to make sure Taterhead had shown up at all he went to the door and knocked. "Yes," Mrs. Ellis informed him, "he was here. In fact you just missed him. He left about 10 minutes ago."

"Thanks," Gaitlin said, gimping down the back porch steps with his cane as fast as he could and hurrying to his car.

Pulling out of the driveway and rapidly accelerating, Gaitlin thought maybe he could still catch up with him. With that old pickup of his and a load of eggs, he was sure that instead of the highway Tater would take the West Blacktop south where he could drive as slow as he wanted.

Sure enough, south of town he spotted Taterhead's battered old red Ford pickup. But it was off the road in the ditch, the load of eggs in disarray. That's strange, Gaitlin thought, wondering what happened. His first inclination was to turn and head back to town, but a gut feeling urged him on instead. Two miles ahead he caught a glimpse of Weasel's old Chrysler disappearing between the tall weeds and brush that lined the dirt trail along the tracks to Schlockrod's pond.

Taterhead must be with Weasel, Gaitlin thought. But that was odd. Why would he abandon his truck at the roadside with a load of eggs to get in Weasel's car and go down to the swimming hole? Gaitlin didn't know but he was going to find out.

At the footpath he found Weasel's sagging old green dinosaur Chrysler - and Axl's red pickup. Gaitlin got out, fumbled with his cane before quietly pushing his door to, shoved his glasses back on his nose and hobbled down the trail for the pond.

Bullets and Fat Bart each had one of Taterhead's arms twisted around behind the trunk of the big old cottonwood while Axl, using his good right side, had hunkered down with the bulk of his weight against the boy's legs and feet. Thus held fast, Weasel was awkwardly attempting to coil the rope around Taterhead and the tree, but all the assistants kept getting in the way as their prey, grunting with the effort, struggled to escape.

Taterhead had fought hard and desperately, Gaitlin saw immediately. His nose and mouth were swollen and bloody and his eyes were black and blue and puffy. One brow was split and bleeding.

Gaitlin stopped at the mouth of the trail, legs apart, most of his weight settled on the ball of his left foot. With the cane firmly planted under his right hand, he drew the pistol with his left just as Axl, Weasel, Bullets and Fat Bart looked up. Nervous Nate had missed the party on account of work.

"Okay assholes, let 'em go!"   Gaitlin ordered sharply, aiming the pistol straight at Fat Bart's head because that was the best shot furthest from Taterhead.

They all looked up and just stood there frozen, unblinking, like statues in a wax museum.

"Let 'em go or I'll blow your fuckin' head off," Gaitlin said evenly, staring straight down the barrel at Fat Bart, the big semiautomatic pistol held steady as a rock.

"You do that," Axl said quietly, looking up from where he was hunched on the ground at Tater's feet, "and you'll spend the rest of your life behind bars."

"With pleasure,"   Gaitlin shifted his gaze to Axl. "Because you'll be the very next to go and Bullets and the Weasel after you, and then the world will be a better place." He returned his gaze to Fat Bart, closed one eye in taking aim and said simply, "Goodbye, fatso."

"No, wait!" Fat Bart blubbered, suddenly releasing Tater and staggering backwards, where he slipped on the muddy bank and fell flat on his back with a loud *smack*.

Taterhead's arm went off like a catapult when Fat Bart let go, and with Axl holding his feet, he put his whole lithe, wiry body into it, busting Bullets' nose with a hammer blow that landed dead center and knocked him ass-backwards into the pond. Like a high-speed precision machine, he then turned on Axl, pummeling either side of the man's face bloody until, panicked, the big buffalo of a human crawled away shouting, "Stop! Stop!"

Deciding not to wait around for his share, Weasel jumped into the pond.

"Okay, Tater, let's go," Gaitlin said, quickly shoving the gun in his jacket and hobbling off up the trail. He was getting faster - and using his right side a whole lot more. Indeed, his leg was making a comeback. He could feel it.

Tossing his cane in the car as Taterhead jumped in the passenger side, Gaitlin slipped behind the wheel, fired her up, backed around and raised dust heading for the blacktop. Taterhead was laughing all the way.   "God, Gaitlin!"   he exclaimed,   "I never been so glad to see someone in my whole life!"

Gaitlin chuckled as he downshifted and turned north, hitting the asphalt and burning rubber for Tater's truck.   "They were gonna castrate you, weren't they?"   Gaitlin looked at his friend.

Turning to stare out the windshield with unseeing eyes, Taterhead heaved a sigh and nodded.   "Yeah.   Something like that."   After a moment he added,   "They tried once before but my friends from Rockford saved me."   He looked at Gaitlin.   "How'd you know?"

Gaitlin lifted a shoulder,   "I didn't know.   But it's what he's always threatened from the beginning."   He pulled to the side across from Taterhead's truck and shut off the engine.

"God, did that feel good bustin' *them* in the chops!"   Taterhead grinned.

"Before I forget, where're you staying down in Rockford?"

After Taterhead explained he added,   "You won't have any trouble finding me, 'cause I'm the only white kid in the neighborhood!"

Gaitlin chuckled.   "What are you gonna do now?"

Taterhead shrugged,   "Go to work, I guess.   I don't think any of my eggs even got broke when they ran me off the road, and I can get cleaned up at my friend's house down in Rockford. His mom's a great cook,"   he added.

"What about them guys?"

"What about them?"

"Well they're probably not done trying."

There was a long silence before Taterhead said, "I don't know, Gaitlin, I guess all I can do is try to avoid them."

Gaitlin pulled out the pistol. "Here, maybe you should take this."

Tater shook his head. "Nah, I ain't no good with a gun. And with your game right side you probably need it more than I do now anyway."

Gaitlin nodded and shoved the gun back in his inner jacket pocket. "Yeah, I suppose you're right about that," he sighed. "Well, now that I know where you're at maybe I'll come down and visit one of these days."

"Do it, Gaitlin," Taterhead said. "It'll be a good time. We'll go have a beer someplace like the old days."

"Sure," Gaitlin replied as they clasped hands in farewell. "I'll surprise you one day."

"Okay, Gaitlin," Taterhead said, climbing out of the car, "and thanks again."

"No problem. I know you'd do the same for me."

Gaitlin watched as Taterhead walked across the road and got in his truck, waited to make sure he wasn't stuck in the ditch, and then headed out to the highway and turned west to a crossroads he knew about with a convenience store that carried beer. It was certainly time for one. And it was only 8:00 o'clock in the morning.

OTHER DREAMS

TWENTY-EIGHT

COLLISION COURSE

"Come on, Colleen, can't we at least have dinner before you leave for the weekend?" Rory Calhoun asked. A fair, handsome lad with blond hair and blue eyes, at 17 he was a year younger than Colleen. A child genius of sorts, he had graduated high school a year early. Having met previously at freshmen orientation, they'd only been going out a week.

"I'd love to have dinner with you, Rory," Colleen O'Brien answered, brushing aside a wisp of bright auburn hair and blinking her striking green eyes, "but I want to get home before dark."

"Why?" Rory teased, "scared the boogie man's gonna get you?"

"No," she shook her head. "It's my headlights. There's something wrong with them."

"What?"

"I don't know," she shrugged. "Every time I hit a bump they go out, then when I hit another bump they come back on. There's no way I can drive after dark like that."

"Well let's take a look. Maybe I can fix it," Rory volunteered with a grin. "I didn't graduate valedictorian for nothing, ya know. Open the hood."

Rory found the problem immediately. One headlight was simply burned out, and on the other, some bozo had cracked the plastic retainer ring that held the halogen bulb firmly seated in the socket. Probably tried forcing it the wrong way with a screw driver when changing the bulb or something.

Rory leaned around the raised hood and called to Colleen sitting behind the wheel, "C'mere!"

Colleen got out and came around the front. "What?"

"See?" he showed her, wiggling the part as the one good headlight flashed on and off. "On this one the retainer ring's cracked, the other headlight's just burned out."

"Well how much will that cost?" Colleen asked with concern.

"Nothing," Rory smiled the smile of the enlightened. "For now, anyway. I'll just tape it up temporarily so you can get home tonight. Then when you get the chance you can go down to Toyota and get a new retainer ring and another bulb for the other light. Probably won't be more than a couple of bucks for the retainer ring," he shrugged.

"You sure that's all that's wrong with it?" Colleen asked warily.

"Sure I'm sure. Look, I'll run up to my room, get the tape, fix the thing, and then we'll test it on our way to dinner."

"On the bumpiest road we can find?"

"Sure," he answered confidently. "If it goes out even once we'll call off dinner and you can leave right away."

The road test had been a complete success and the dinner hour well past when Colleen finally kissed her first true love goodbye for the weekend. In fact it was pushing 9:00 o'clock when she dropped him off outside his dorm and headed north for home.

Remembering about the roadblock every Friday night on Route 32 east of town, Colleen decided to get off I-39 south of Rockford and take the West Blacktop north into Harlot to skirt it.

Not because she had been drinking, but simply to avoid the inconvenience and delay. Sometimes they made you get out of the car while they conducted a thorough search and ran a computer check on your ID.

*   *   *

Gaitlin Tyler was drinking. In fact he had an open one wedged between his seat and the console. He had something to celebrate. It was his first night going without his cane. He still had a limp, of course, but his right leg was coming back fast and he'd been mobile on both legs all day.

Feeling lonely and lost and with nowhere to go on a Friday night, on the spur of the moment he decided to run down to Rockford and look up Taterhead. Of course avoiding the roadblock was his first priority. At the West Blacktop he turned south for Rockford and gunned the little four-banger Dodge with the driver's side air bag.

*   *   *

Taking a long, sucking drag on the joint, Bullets said tightly while struggling to hold it in, "Yeah, it's pretty good." Handing the joint off to Weasel, he asked, "What do you think?"

Nodding his approval, Weasel took a noisy drag. "Yeah, it's pretty good," he said, flipping the roach into the ash tray. "It's cashed."

"Okay, I'll take a quarter," Bullets said to the kid in the back seat.

"Yeah man, it's kick-ass," the 15-year-old said, extending a rolled-up plastic baggy containing a green leafy substance between the front bucket seats. It looked like some kind of weird space-age cigar.

Bullets took the baggy, slipped it into the pocket of his denim jacket and reached behind him with a roll of bills. "Okay?"

Quickly snatching the cash and counting it, the kid answered, "Yeah, sure. Any time."

"All right, then," Bullets said, flipping the door open and leaning forward so the kid could get out. "See you next time, okay?"

"Sure," the kid answered as he climbed out of the back. "I always got good stuff."

"All right," Bullets grinned, extending his hand palm up. They slapped five and then the kid turned on his heel and vanished into the dreary darkness that enveloped one of Rockford's urban parks.

"What now?" Weasel asked.

Pulling the baggy from his pocket, Bullets tossed it to him, saying, "Now you'll twist one up for the road while I get us out of here."

"What about the roadblock on Route 32?"

"Don't matter," Bullets replied, "we'll just take the West Blacktop north and go around the bastards."

OTHER DREAMS

TWENTY-NINE

HOT RUBBER COLD CHICKEN

"It's a girl," Weasel insisted.

"No it's not," Bullets countered just as adamantly, "it's a guy with long hair. You done rolling that joint yet?" he added irritably, shooting him a glance.

"Gimme a break, I'm working on it."

"My sister just got a Toyota," Bullets said, suddenly chatty from the glow of his high. He hadn't even seen the car before she'd gone off to school in it. He had always been gone or in bed when she was home during the week before she left.

"Maybe that's her," Weasel said, rolling the ends of the joint between his lips.

"Nah," Bullets shook his head. "She wouldn't be driving so slow. No one in our family does. Besides, like I told ya, that's a guy with long hair."

"No way," Weasel argued, lighting up the illicit smoke, "but whatever it is, you're following too close."

"That's because I'm going to pass," Bullets replied as they dipped through a fog-shrouded valley.

"Not on a hill."

"Yes, on a hill. My car has balls, buddy, watch this. . . ."

*   *   *

If the genius had used electrical tape the temporary repair job might have lasted more than 45 minutes. But he didn't have any electrical tape and was anxious to spend a little free time with the first true love of his life.

Big mistake. The intense heat of the engine compartment and the hot halogen lamp quickly dried and cracked the scotch tape he *had* used and now Colleen was creeping along at 40 miles-an-hour hoping her lights wouldn't go out again. And some idiot was tailgating her. Well, he would just have to wait for a passing zone.

But he didn't. And just as he made his move, a bump in the road knocked her headlights out. . . .

*   *   *

Gaitlin couldn't believe it. As he crested the hill at a mellow 60 miles-an-hour an oncoming car suddenly swerved into his lane and was coming straight at him. A nut? A suicide case? Someone playing chicken?

At a combined closing speed of roughly 140 MPH, that was it. Seven seconds and three thoughts later he'd used up all the highway that time and space allowed. Gaitlin had to move. For a second he thought he saw the amber marker lights of another vehicle in the northbound lane, but the fog made them seem more like distant reflectors to mark a driveway. Impulsively he swerved left, directly into the path of a ton-and-a-half of glass, plastic, and steel that he never saw, for a combined impact-speed of 100 MPH.

OTHER DREAMS

THIRTY

HELL ON WHEELS

He was suffocating. He couldn't move. It was like a nightmare he once had when he was trying to run but his legs wouldn't. And then whatever was pressing against his face and chest with such smothering force shriveled away and he was sucking wind again.

The air was heavy and thick and misty around him. He kept thinking it was such a strange nightmare because it was so real. But it couldn't be. He was in some strange world made up of crumpled, sharp edges and there was a small hole at one end aglow with a swirling, hazy mist. He reached up and felt for his glasses. Amazing. They were right where they were supposed to be. In a dazed stupor, all he knew was that to be safe he somehow had to get to the hole and crawl out.

That was funny. The hole wasn't nearly so far away as he'd thought. And this wasn't such a bad nightmare. At least all his arms and legs seemed to work okay. But this wasn't his bed, either, he realized with surprise as he crawled on his hands and knees across something hard, warm and gritty. In fact it felt, and in some vague way smelled, like asphalt. And cars. And gasoline.

Suffering from severe shock, half-blind and seeing through a long, dark tunnel of thick, swirling fog, Gaitlin decided to try standing.   Swaying like a drunkard, he carefully got to his feet and. . . what the hell was *it?* An alien spaceship?

It looked like a crumpled ball of blue aluminum foil, and inside was a strange alien life form, greenish and glittering and making a very slight crunching, grating sound as it moved oh so slightly in and out - as if the glittering green thing was a breathing lung.

Gaitlin just stood there utterly mesmerized. What the hell was it? Wait! It. . . it had a *wig,* for Christ's sake! Long, auburn hair. And it looked like the glittering green alien was trying to *eat* the wig!

Colleen would have been catapulted clear through the windshield but the tremendous impact pushed the dashboard backwards and down, in effect snatching her back into the car even as the steering wheel rammed down into her lap and pinched both her legs off as easily as a child pulling the legs off a spider.

It left her head buried in the windshield to the bridge of her nose. And even as the spider's legs, though completely detached, continue crawling about, so this human organism, in its death throes continued to squirm and jerk spasmodically against the powerful force holding it fast.

The powerful force, a plastic-impregnated safety glass windshield, grating and grinding with the movement of the trapped organism, finally won, sucking the top of her head off and leaving behind a mass of red, quivering gelatinous matter that for all the world reminded Gaitlin of chopped liver. The glittering green membrane-like lung, apparently satisfied with the wig, went curiously still. But something was hanging from the side of the crumpled blue ball. . . .

It looked like a human arm complete with a hand and five fingers at the end of it. Nah, couldn't be, Gaitlin's shock-dulled brain told him as he took a wobbly step forward and peered closely But it was, cleanly severed at the shoulder and hanging by a sleeve from one sharp point of the crumpled aluminum-foil ball.

And then Gaitlin was on his knees with gut-wrenching heaves of acrid vomit. Oh God, No! No! Vomit drooled down his chin and sprayed out his nose as he fell back on his heels shrieking and crying with strangled curses of protest that echoed to the heavens. Because all at once he knew. This was no nightmare. This was reality. And it was all his.

OTHER DREAMS

THIRTY-ONE

A STATE CALLED DENIAL

"Who is it?" Bullets mumbled through eyes still puffy with sleep. His head was pounding and felt big as a watermelon. He had passed out at Weasel's in a beer-and-marijuana-induced stupor the night before.

"It's your dad," Weasel said, feeling pretty queasy himself. Although 9:00 o'clock in the morning, it was still more than four hours before either normally woke up, the incessant ringing of the telephone having dragged both out of complete oblivion.

"Tell him I'm not here," Bullets mumbled again and rolled over, snuggling under the blanket.

"I can't, I already told him you were here," Weasel said. "Besides, he sounds pretty upset."

"Shit," is all Bullets said. With a supreme effort he bounded off the couch and wobbled for the kitchen and the phone while Weasel, with sudden urgency, hurried to the john to pay homage to the porcelain god.

Grabbing the receiver off the counter where Weasel had left it, Bullets asked rather irritably, "What, dad?" His dad knew damn well he never got up before noon.

All traces of irritation quickly disappeared as he asked several questions, promised to be home soon and hung up.

Turning to Weasel, who came wandering into the kitchen belching and farting, all he said was, "My sister's dead."

Weasel froze in his tracks, eyes growing wide. "Dead?"

Bullets slowly nodded.

"How. . . who?"

"Car wreck," Bullets almost whispered.

Neither had actually witnessed the collision. At 90-miles-an-hour and climbing, both had been stoned to the bone and staring straight ahead, mesmerized by the headlights eating up the road. They had blasted over the crest of the hill and out of sight even as the Dodge and Toyota slammed into each other with a force that scattered pieces of automobile clear into the cornfields.

"Do you think it was her in that car we passed last night?"

"No way," Bullets quickly answered, adding, "that was a guy. And even if it *was* her, the accident must have happened way after we passed her."

"What'd she hit?" Weasel asked, crossing to the sink and turning the cold water on full-force.

"Gaitlin Tyler," Bullets answered, his eyes following Weasel's every move.

About to drink straight off the tap, Weasel stopped and looked up. *"Gaitlin?"* he squinted. "Well what happened to him?"

"Nothin', I guess. He's in the hospital, but my dad said he wasn't even hurt. At least that's what the police told him."

"Do you think it was. . . ."

"No way," Bullets sharply interjected, adding tightly in words spoken slowly and precisely, "We didn't *see* no accident last night."

"I know," Weasel quickly responded, "but what about that other. . . . "

"Just forget about it!" Bullets angrily exploded, "will you?"

Staring wide-eyed, Weasel slowly nodded, adding, "Sure, Bullets. I mean, what's there to forget, anyway? We didn't see no accident or nothin'."

"I know that," Bullets said absently, giving Weasel the distinct impression that he really *had* already forgotten.

Looking haggard, *grief stricken over the loss of his sister?* Bullets shuffled almost painfully to the refrigerator and opened the door to peer inside, asking in a voice heavy with despair, "Any beer left?"

OTHER DREAMS

THIRTY-TWO

RUNNING THE GAUNTLET

The seat belt, and especially the air bag, had saved Gaitlin's life. In fact he was left virtually unscathed - physically at least. The psychological torture, visions of the horror scene and Colleen's gruesome death he would endure for the rest of his life. Nightmares.

But none of this was on Gaitlin's mind as, manacled hand-and-foot, he was driven to the county court house for his first hearing. Looking frail and thin and white as a ghost after having spent three weeks in the county lockup, Gaitlin was led by deputies to the court house doors through a gauntlet of screaming protesters spitting in his face and calling him a murderer.

Largely made up of Renee Cooley's MAID organization (Mothers Against Intoxicated Drivers), they carried big signs emblazoned with various messages like GAITLIN TYLER IS A MURDERER; or, A FATALITY INVOLVING DRUNK DRIVING IS PREMEDITATED MURDER; and, PUT HIM AWAY FOR LIFE OR YOUR CHILD COULD BE NEXT; Anna O'Brien carried one reading simply, GAITLIN TYLER MURDERED MY DAUGHTER.

Gaitlin Tyler's blood alcohol level, taken at the scene, had come in at exactly 0.10, a county officer testified at the hearing.

Right on the line, he was technically, and for the purposes of prosecution, legally drunk at the time of the fatal collision.

After that had been quickly and easily established the judge informed Gaitlin that he was charged with reckless homicide and asked how he was pleading.

Gaitlin was tempted to plead guilty and get the whole thing over with as quickly as possible. After all, as far as he was concerned his life was over. And he *did* feel guilty.

But his court appointed attorney, in frantic whispers, insisted that, as with most things in life, this was only a little game that must be played out. With a sigh, Gaitlin gave in and pled innocent as instructed. The judge then set the trial date - for exactly one month from the day.

OTHER DREAMS

THIRTY-THREE

A GOOD COP GOES TO WORK

No one saw much of Bullets and Weasel anymore. They were always off alone somewhere - just the two of them. Good for nothing drunk 99 percent of the time and the other one percent nursing severe hangovers, the one time Axl ran into them during the last three weeks, at the Gray Wolf Tap when they were picking up a case of beer, they were both so much bleary-eyed beer-swollen stench that the conversation lasted about 15 seconds - and then Axl returned to his bar stool and hunched down over his brew.

With those two out of the picture and himself still nursing broken bones, sexually mutilating Taterhead would have to be put on hold for awhile. At least until he was fully recovered. Then he'd have to work out a good plan. As the saying goes, if you want something done right, you gotta do it yourself. . .

Everyone assumed Bullets' and Weasel's drunken withdrawal from society was merely a grieving brother nursing the wounded loss of a beloved sister, and the loyal friend who stood by to help carry the pain and offer comfort. In reality it had more to do with a couple of snakes nursing guilty consciences.

In any case, Taterhead found it safer to be out and about now, what with the community's outrage presently directed at the survivor of Harlot's latest tragedy. And with the disappearance of Bullets and Weasel from the scene, and Axl's own apparent withdrawal, he was spending a lot more time at home attending to business, reading books about cheese-making, and preparing to buy a cow. He even felt safe enough to make a trip to the county lockup and visit Gaitlin, which at first he was afraid to do simply because he didn't want to attract additional animosity from the community-at-large.

George and Marybell Tyler simply didn't have the money to bail their son out of jail. Neither did Taterhead. But on his visit he was shocked at his friend's appearance. Gaitlin was literally wasting away, his face thin, drawn and deeply lined. He looked like he'd aged 10 years.

Weren't they feeding him? Taterhead joked, managing to draw Gaitlin out of his lethargy. Attempting to get the wheels of Gaitlin's memory turning again, Taterhead asked on a more serious note if, in fact, he *had* been drunk at the time of the collision.

No, not really. He'd had a few beers but it wasn't like he was bombed or out of control or anything.

Then what was he doing all the way over on the wrong side of the road? Why was he driving south in the northbound lane?

Because a northbound car swerved over into *his* lane, Gaitlin patiently explained. Like the guy was playing chicken or something.

"Chicken?"

"I don't know," Gaitlin shrugged.

Taterhead looked perplexed. "Well why didn't you go for the shoulder?"

"Because I thought maybe the guy had fallen asleep or something and might keep drifting over the way he'd started in the first place and hit the shoulder at the same time as me. So I went for the best opening I saw. You gotta remember, this is all going down over a matter of seconds."

"Wait!" Taterhead almost stood up. "The best opening you saw was *head on into another car?* That don't make sense!"

"But there was no other car!" Gaitlin heatedly insisted. And then it hit like a torpedo - the other car had switched off its headlights just as the first car pulled over into his lane!

Shaking his head in disbelief at the sudden realization, Gaitlin exclaimed, "That *has* to be it! I don't know what I was thinking at the time. Like I said, everything was happening so fast, but maybe I thought the car that switched off its headlights had pulled into a driveway or something - I only had a split-second to react, don't forget."

Deep in thought, Taterhead nodded. Now things were starting to make sense. At least a little. He looked up. "Colleen's a pretty sharp girl, top of her class and all. Why would she suddenly shut off her headlights in the pitch dark at 9:00 o'clock at night with one car passing and southbound traffic dead ahead? It don't make sense."

As mystified as anyone, Gaitlin shook his head and shrugged.

*   *   *

Taterhead left the lockup, marched straight over to the administration building and went up to the front counter. "Is officer Rankin in?" he asked.

"One moment and I'll check," the dispatcher replied.

Not only was Rankin in, but he agreed to see Taterhead immediately. "Right through that door and down the hall and he'll be waiting for you," the dispatcher instructed, buzzing him through the security door.

Taterhead grabbed the big knob and shoved through as the heavy bolt electronically snapped aside. Rankin was at the end of the hall. "Tater!" he smiled, beckoning with a wave of his arm, "glad you came by."

He showed Taterhead into a cramped office he shared with two other county deputies, both out at the time, went behind his desk and motioned for Taterhead to take the straight-back wooden chair in front. "What can I do for you, son?" the veteran officer asked, coming straight to the point.

"It's about Gaitlin," Taterhead began in earnest, "I think there's more to this story than meets the eye."

"So do I," Rankin agreed at once. "And the thing that's been bugging me ever since I investigated the accident scene is the fact that Gaitlin hadn't simply screwed up and wandered over the center line a little bit because of too much drinking or digging through his glove box or something. He was fully all the way over, completely occupying the northbound lane."

"I know, and there's a good reason for it," Taterhead excitedly interrupted the man.

"Do tell," Rankin encouraged, settling back to listen with interest as Taterhead explained.

When the boy finished, Rankin heaved a big, thoughtful sigh and said, "But there's one thing about all this that doesn't make sense. Colleen O'Brien was a sharp little girl. Much too sophisticated and intelligent to shut off her headlights like that."

"I agree," Taterhead looked at the man. "So what's it mean?"

"Only one of two things," Rankin pondered. "Either she wasn't as sharp as we think, meaning, namely, that she was playing games. . . ."

"Or?"

"At a critical moment, like just when this other mystery car pulled out to pass, her headlights failed."

"Maybe if we examined the headlight system."

Rankin looked doubtful. "The car was so completely demolished it'd be pretty hard to find any evidence there. But maybe, just maybe, if she was having some problems with the headlight system, she talked to someone down at school about it before leaving."

"Like who?" Taterhead asked with growing interest.

"Well, a good place to start would be to talk to her roommate at the dorms she was staying in."

Taterhead sat back with a smile as Rankin grabbed the phone and quickly dialed.

After a brief conversation with the deceased's father in which he quickly jotted down some notes, he hung up. "Now we're getting somewhere," he said, glancing at Taterhead briefly and holding up a finger as he quickly dialed a second time.

During the course of the conversation with Colleen's ex-roommate he learned two important facts. Yes, the roommate confirmed, Colleen *had* mentioned some trouble with her headlights. But more importantly, as far as Rankin was concerned, the last person to see her alive was a new boyfriend, Rory Calhoun, who, according to the girl, seemed to have developed an extreme guilt complex about Colleen's death - as if somehow it had been all his fault. Rankin thanked the girl and hung up.

Hand still on the phone, he stared at Taterhead for a long moment, then shoved his chair back and stood up, saying brusquely, "Let's go!"

"Where?" Taterhead asked, leaping from his chair and quickly following the big veteran police officer as he plodded down the hall.

"To NIU, lad, we've got to talk to one Rory Calhoun."

*   *   *

"Certainly," the young coed behind the reception counter smiled, looked up the number in her listings and pointed to the house phone. "It's 9996."

"Thank you," Rankin said and turned to the phone. Dialing the number, he glanced at Taterhead and said, "I just hope he's here."

Rory Calhoun answered on the third ring. He sounded listless and disoriented to Rankin, but he agreed to meet with the officer and told him to come up.

Locating his room on the ninth floor, they found the door ajar. It opened with a squeak as Rankin lightly tapped on it.

Rory Calhoun was sitting on the edge of his desk staring out the window. "Come in," he said without turning.

"Rory Calhoun?" Rankin inquired softly.

"Yes?" the boy turned his gaze on Rankin and Taterhead.

He looked like he still belonged in high school, Rankin thought. "Could we ask you a few questions?"

"Yes," the boy answered, his voice trembling.

With fear or emotion? The boy sure looked a mess. Like he'd been crying for weeks. "I understand you were the last person to see Colleen on the Friday before she left for home - the weekend she was involved in a fatal collision?"

"Yes," the boy's voice shook again as he turned back to the window.

"Her roommate said she'd been having some trouble with her headlights." Rankin paused. "Can you tell us anything about that?"

Still facing the window, all at once he broke down, his shoulders shaking as he sobbed into his hands.

In three big strides Rankin crossed the room and placed a gentle hand on the boy's shoulder. "Look," he said softly, "it's not your fault."

"Yes it is!" the boy wailed, twisting around to look at Rankin, the tears flowing freely. "It *is* my fault! All my fault!"

"But why?" Rankin frowned. And here he took a shot in the dark, "Were. . . were you in another car that pulled out to pass?"

"No," Rory sniffled, shaking his head. "I'm the stupid jerk that fixed her headlights," and once again he broke down with sobs that racked his whole body.

Taterhead stood frozen at the open door, one hand on the knob. Rankin turned to him with a forefinger to his lips, then turned back to Rory and waited in absolute silence until the boy's sobbing subsided and he turned to look.

"What was wrong with her headlights?" Rankin asked softly.

Sniffling, Rory wiped at his nose with the back of his hand but didn't accomplish much. Rankin snatched a tissue from a box of kleenex on the desk and handed it to him, repeating the question, "What was wrong with her headlights, Rory?"

Rory blew his nose and shrugged, saying in a tiny, high voice, "Well, one was burned out and the other," he paused and looked up at the big man, "the other, the plastic retainer ring was cracked."

Rory was about to break down again but Rankin pulled him back, jostling him with a firm, gentle hand on his shoulder and coaxing, "Come on now, Rory, you might be able to help another boy that's in serious trouble. Would you help us?"

Rory looked up at Rankin and blinked through his tears. "Yes," he answered in a small voice.

"Okay, what about the plastic retainer ring?"

The boy hesitated, sniffling. Rankin snatched another tissue and handed it to him. After the boy blew his nose a second time and dabbed at his eyes with a sleeve, he continued in a stronger voice. "Well, the retainer ring was cracked and every time she hit a bump in the road her headlights would go out, so I taped it up with scotch tape." the boy's voice broke again as he gulped air, then regained his composure with a shivery sigh that

caused his whole body to tremble. "I - I know what happened,"
he stammered, blinking up at the big officer.

"What? What happened?" Rankin asked softly.

"The heat under the hood, or the lights or whatever, dried
out the tape and it cracked." Heaving a huge shaky sigh, he
slumped in defeat, murmuring almost to himself, "I should've
used electrical tape. . . ."

After allowing a quiet, reflective moment to pass, Rankin
asked curiously, "Do you know if there was another car? I
mean, like, someone else from school or home or whatever that
was supposed to follow her back to Harlot?"

Once again having turned to the window, the boy silently
shook his head. "No. Not that I know of. She was supposed to
drive up alone. Left some time after nine."

Bingo! Everything jibed. Including the boy's testimony
as to what time she'd left the University, and especially the part
about her headlights. "Look at me," Rankin said evenly. The
boy turned and stared at Rankin unblinking. "Would you be
willing to testify to all this in a court of law?"

Rory Calhoun slowly nodded, insisting, "It's the truth,
sir, every word. I swear."

"I believe you, son. Otherwise I wouldn't have asked you
to testify."

At the door Rankin turned and said, "Hey, Rory?"

"Yeah?" Once again the boy turned from his perch at the
window.

"Forget about the guilt-trip. Yeah, you made a mistake,
but it was only one small, contributing factor in a series of sad
incidents that led to the accident. It's *not* your fault. You're
intelligent, a good kid, the world could use more like you, but not
if you go off the deep end, okay?"

Rory managed a weak smile. "Okay."

Driving back to Harlot, Rankin turned to Taterhead and
said seriously, *"Now* let's go take a look at Colleen's car."

"But I thought you said. . . ."

"Now that we know what we're looking for," Rankin shrugged, "you never know, maybe this plastic headlight part is intact with a little piece of that scotch tape still stuck to it. If so, we'll shoot some photo's and then take the part with us. It won't in itself make or break our case of course, but with Rory's testimony it'll sure look good in court."

*   *   *

"They ever find that red car that run me off the road?" Jed Holiday, of Jed's Junkyard and Salvage asked the moment Rankin and Taterhead walked through the door of the cement-block building. It was the first question he asked Rankin every time he saw him.

"No, Jed, they didn't," Rankin replied tediously, "but we would like to take a look at Colleen O'Brien's car."

Noting the camera in Rankin's hand, Jed commented with surprise, "More pictures? Every cop and prosecutor in the county must'a been by here five times now takin' pictures!"

"Then one more time won't matter much, will it?" Rankin smiled.

"Hey," old Jed shrugged, "you're the law. If you wanna take pictures, welcome to it. She's out back - you know where."

"Thanks, Jed," Rankin said, leading the way as he and Tater pushed through the swing door at the end of the counter and headed out back.

Both cars were sitting side by side out behind the cement-block building. Almost everyone in the county had seen the cars - several times. But every time Taterhead saw them he was amazed all over again.

Colleen's car looked like a crumpled ball of blue foil. Gaitlin's car, at point of impact moving almost 30 miles-an-hour faster, had gone up over the top. This, along with the seat belt and air bag, of course, was undoubtedly a major factor in Gaitlin walking away from the accident with scarcely a bruise or a cut, while the tremendous impact had rammed Colleen's car into an accordion, the front bumper nearly touching the back, as if the little Toyota had been put in a machine press.   The nose of Gaitlin's car, on the other hand, had folded under, popping the windshield out and providing the "hole" through which he had escaped.

Taterhead let out a long, low whistle, commenting, "We're not going to find anything in *that!*"

"Don't be too sure," Rankin said, camera in hand as he walked over to the crumpled ball of steel that had once been Colleen's Toyota.

All that remained of the Toyota's headlights was a single tiny shard of glass attached to a small black plastic cylindrical socket hanging by its wires, but Rankin found it immediately.

"Well what'a ya know,"   he grinned, looking at Taterhead. "C'mere."

Taterhead walked up to where Rankin was leaning over the wreckage. The big man pointed. "You see that?"

Taterhead leaned over, peering closely. And there it was, the socket with the cracked retainer ring, a single wisp of yellowed, dried scotch tape still clinging to it.

"Step back," Rankin ordered. He quickly snapped several pictures from various angles and distances, handed Tater the camera and slipped a pen knife out of his pocket. Working carefully in hopes of removing the socket without knocking off the piece of scotch tape, Rankin severed the wires, carefully placed the part, shard, cracked retainer ring, scotch tape and all in a plastic sandwich bag, folded it into his pocket and said evenly, "Let's go."

"What about the mystery car?" Taterhead asked as they got in the squad car and slammed the doors.

Starting the engine, Rankin shrugged, asking, "Got any ideas?" Without waiting for an answer he backed around and headed north on the blacktop for Harlot.

Tater pondered for some moments, then shook his head. "Not really," he paused, "but I've heard Bullets and Weasel have been acting mighty strange lately."

Rankin looked at the kid. It was just a hunch - but one they both shared. After a moment he said, "Nah, he's just broke up over his sister gettin' killed is all."

"Hmmm," Tater reflected, slightly shaking his head, "they weren't that close."

OTHER DREAMS

THIRTY-FOUR

TWO CREEPS AND A COP

After thanking Taterhead for his help and dropping him off at the lockup where the boy had left his truck, Rankin roared off for Harlot. There were two boys he wanted to talk to, and he had a pretty good idea where he could find them, too.

Rankin had spotted Bullets' blue Torino at Weasel's a lot lately, and it was there when he wheeled the big police cruiser into the driveway behind it and shut down the engine. No one was going anywhere without first talking to him.

He rapped on the door, then a second time louder. After a third series of loud raps he heard the lock being rattled. A moment later the door opened a crack. Bleary-eyed, stinking of beer and obviously drunk, Weasel peered out at him, asking in his typically amiable way, "What's up?"

Rankin lifted a shoulder, "I was wondering if I could talk to you boys for a minute."

After a moment's hesitation Weasel said, "Yeah, sure, be right out," and closed the door.

Wondering just what the hell was going on inside, Rankin left the small porch of the tiny one bedroom shack and leaned against the fender of his cruiser, ankles crossed and arms folded across his chest.

And they let him wait a good long time, too, before emerging from the tiny wood framed structure, each clutching a bottle of beer and looking unsteady as hell. This was going to be easy. And that was Rankin's first mistake.

"What's up?" Weasel repeated his favorite phrase.

Rankin eyed them sternly for some moments before turning his gaze on Bullets and saying evenly, "Sorry about your sister, Bullets."

"Yeah, yeah, sure, I heard it a thousand times by now, but thanks."

"Got some new info on the accident that killed her," Rankin said pointblank. Watching both boys closely, he added, "We got a new witness says there was a third car there when the accident happened, but it fled the scene."

Startled, both boys looked at one another with the unspoken accusation of betrayal. Someone had talked, and as they were both acutely aware, there were only two people on the planet who were in that third car - and they were both staring at each other.

None of this was lost on Rankin, of course, but then he made his second mistake. If he had just waited, the truth would have unravelled before his eyes. But instead he played his hunch, an erroneous one, and bore in on Weasel, saying evenly, "The witness thought it was a big old green Chrysler," he paused, pointing at Weasel's car in the driveway before adding softly, "like that one there."

Both boys immediately breathed easier, Weasel slowly shaking his head and saying with sudden, bold confidence, "Well it wasn't this old Chrysler here, sir. It was sitting right here in the driveway the whole night of Colleen's accident - I was with Bullets." He shrugged. "Ask my neighbors."

Rankin left cursing himself all the way back to headquarters. He knew the truth. It was Bullets. But so what?

He was the *only* one who knew. And it meant absolutely nothing.
He had no proof.

OTHER DREAMS

THIRTY-FIVE

SETTING A RAT TRAP

Officer Hal Rankin of the Jefferson County Sheriff's Police got up early the following morning. He knew where to find Taterhead Ellis - at his folks' house tending the chickens and collecting eggs for the marketplace in Rockford.

He arrived at the Ellis place at 6:00 AM sharp and sure enough, Taterhead's pickup was in the drive near the barn. Rankin pulled up next to the battered old Ford, got out and went around to the chicken coop where he found Taterhead in the wire mesh enclosure tossing feed to the chickens and absently humming Ozzy Osborne's *Suicide Solution.*

The boy looked up with surprise as the big officer crunched through the dry, overgrown grass and stopped at the gate. "Mr. Rankin," is all he said.

"Tater," the man gave a single nod and touched the brim of his Stetson. He paused, looking grim as he admitted, "I screwed up big time yesterday afternoon - and that's the bad news."

"What's the good news?" Taterhead asked, tossing a last handful of feed to the chickens and hanging the bucket on a nail under the eave of the coop.

"The good news is, I know who was driving the mystery car."

"Who?" Taterhead asked, picking up the large cane basket he used for collecting the eggs.

"Bullets," Rankin answered, "but I tipped my hand too soon and blew it."

"Meaning?"

"Meaning unless I can figure out some way to trick him into admitting the truth in front of a witness or two, he's going to get away with it."

"Oh." Taterhead looked crestfallen, then made a gesture for Rankin to follow and went into the chicken coop.

With a squeak from the pipe and wire mesh gate, Rankin pushed through into the yard, took off the big brown Stetson and ducked into the hen house. "But I think we can still nail him," he continued as Taterhead moved about the musky little shack collecting eggs. "With your help."

At that Taterhead chuckled. "Bullets ain't gonna admit nothing to *me,*" he intoned.

"Not forthrightly, no," Rankin readily agreed, "but if we tricked him. . . ."

"How?" Taterhead stopped and looked at the man.

Rankin's plan was a simple one. The boys always got together for a beer party at Weasel's on Friday night. All Taterhead had to do was show up, and in the course of having a beer, start drawing Bullets and the rest of the revelers in with intimations that he knew there was a third car at the scene of the accident, and just when he had everyone's curiosity aroused, proclaim that it was, in fact, Bullets' car that had fled the scene. How does Taterhead know this? Certainly everyone will want to know. Taterhead's to reply simply that Bullets, along with everyone else, will find out in court.

Staring at the man, Taterhead sank to one of the nesting shelves and set his basket down. Dropping his gaze, he said, "There's something you should know, Mr. Rankin."

Hal Rankin remained silent.

His gaze on the floor, Taterhead admitted with a sigh, "Those guys tried to mutilate me - twice."

After a long, silent moment Rankin nodded, saying softly, "I know, Tater, I know - and that's what I'm counting on."

Taterhead looked up sharply and stared at the man.

"If they're capable of doing that," Rankin went on softly, "they're capable of murder - and now Bullets would have a strong motivation to do just that."

"B-But. . . ." Taterhead stammered in protest.

Rankin silenced him with a raised hand. "Listen." From his pocket he took a small device that looked like a beeper that clipped to a belt. He held it up, explaining, "This is a transmitter." He pushed a button on top and instantly a little beeper clipped to his belt emitted a loud, rapid series of high pitched beeps.

Rankin reached down and switched off the beeper on his belt. Holding up the transmitter again he continued, "This is the only transmitter that'll set off this beeper," he indicated the one clipped to his belt. "When you go in, I'll be standing-by the next block over. Once you do your little charade and Bullets makes up his mind that he's got to get rid of you and incites the others to help, that in itself will implicate him as the one who was at the scene of his sister's fatal collision." Here Rankin paused dramatically. "Then, all you gotta do is push this little button here," he pushed it again which instantly started the one clipped to his belt beeping, "and I come busting in." He reached down and switched off the beeper. "Voila!" he held up his hands, concluding triumphantly, "and now we've got Bullets in the bag!"

Taterhead was flabbergasted. He couldn't believe it. The plan was perfect! And not only that, but if successful it would certainly go a long way towards alleviating his own personal problems with the whole town. But. . . .

Taterhead looked up. "So what? Once we get into court it'll just be my word against four other guy's word about what went on in that house that caused me to signal you to come bustin' in."

At that Rankin smiled hugely and shook his head. "Uh-uh. Yesterday afternoon I went to see judge Thompson, explained the situation, and got a court order allowing me to eaves-drop on this bunch. You'll be wearing a small, electronic microphone transmitting to a little recorder that'll be hidden in the bushes near the door - it'll pick up every word."

At that Taterhead chuckled.

"Then you'll do it?" Rankin asked, anxiously looking on.

Grinning from ear to ear, Taterhead nodded.

OTHER DREAMS

THIRTY-SIX

FUTURE QUEEN OF THE BIG SCREEN

13-year-old Erica Erickson had to keep her mouth shut. She'd lied in the first place to cover up her own offense, minor as it was, but now she was in it up to her neck. Ultimately, though, what difference did it make what happened to Taterhead? He was a queer and should be put to death. The bible said so. So did Pastor Renfrow. And so if all that happened to Taterhead was a little minor surgery on a part he didn't know what to do with anyway, well, as far as she was concerned he was getting off easy. It wasn't her fault he was homo.

All she knew was that it was a warm, balmy Friday night in the midst of Indian Summer, and the call of freedom, whispered on the autumn-scented winds of October, was beckoning. She had to get out.

With all the hysteria and recurrent hysteria, she felt like a prisoner, so watchful were all the adults. At school. At home. At the store and at the corner playground. It was like being under armed guard at all times. Suffocating beneath this blanket of "protection", she decided to escape. It would be her last chance before winter set in.

And she knew where a party was happening. At Weasel's only a block over. He had a party every Friday. She could hear the faint beat of the music from her window. And so at 10:00 o'clock on Friday night with the weekend looming, she told her parents she was going to bed, went to her room, closed the door, turned out the light and carefully and quietly raised her bedroom window. She crept out into the night barefoot and wearing only panties and a nightshirt that hung down to her knees.

*   *   *

As always of late it wasn't much of a party. Bullets, Weasel, Fat Bart and Nervous Nate sat around swigging beer and playing the music too loud. And with the only intimate contact allowed being in a context of violence, they were given to acting silly and jumping on one another in pseudo fights and various contests of strength that left them safe to experience human contact - which they all desperately desired.

Thus were they rolling about on the floor and crashing into furniture when Erica pushed the door open and stopped on the threshold. "Hey, guys!" she exclaimed in a super-heated voice to be heard above the slam bang combat and thump of the music.

Entangled in a major pile-up, they all stopped and looked up for one frozen moment before Bullets pushed a fallen floor lamp off, climbed from the top of the heap and stood up. "Hi, Erica," he said, blinking with happy delirium.

"Hi," she said, flipping the door closed behind her and moving about the room righting overturned chairs as the rest of the boys disentangled themselves and stood up.

"Want a beer, Erica?" Weasel asked.

"Sure," she answered, plopping down on the sofa.

"What're you doing out?" Fat Bart asked.

"Snuck out," she replied. It wasn't the first time she'd climbed out her bedroom window at night to party with the older kids. In fact Kevin Crisper and Johnny Bulger usually snuck out with her.

"Where's your two little boy friends?"   Nervous Nate asked.

"I don't know.   Home I guess," Erica answered, taking a tentative sip of the beer Weasel handed her.   "They got caught last time and can't sneak out for awhile."

"Grab me one, too," Bullets called after Fat Bart, who was heading for the kitchen, then he plopped down on the sofa next to Erica.   Nervous Nate took a spot on the couch on Erica's other side and Weasel pulled up a chair.

Fat Bart returned from the kitchen with the beers, handed Bullets his and likewise pulled up a chair next to Weasel, stretched his legs out on the coffee table and crossed them at the ankles.

The boys were pretty well lit-up already, but it wouldn't take Erica long to catch up.   With no alcohol tolerance, no physical bulk, and with little food in her stomach due to the eternal diet every teenaged girl seemed to be on, three beers later and she was just as loaded as they were, laughing hysterically at everything and babbling incessantly about how she was going to be a rich and famous movie star someday.

"An actress?"   Bullets looked at her with a crooked grin. "What're you gonna do about the nude scenes?"

"What nude scenes?"   Erica giggled.

"The nude scenes.   Every actress has to do nude scenes in the movies.   You know," he went on, "you've seen enough movies."

"So," Erica shrugged with a coy smile, "I'll just do them.   My body's good enough!"

"I bet!"   Nervous Nate hooted.

"You looked real good out there in the street that time with Taterhead!"   Fat Bart grinned.

"Yeah," Weasel put in, "let's see you do a nude scene right now."

"You're gonna need some practice if you're gonna be a star," Bullets looked at her.   "Might as well start right now."

With a childlike laugh Erica exclaimed, "But this isn't a movie!"

"No, but you could, ya know, get up on the table and do a little striptease or something," Bullets coaxed.

"Yeah, Erica, come on," Nervous Nate put in.

Looking around the group of drunken boys anxiously sitting on the edges of their seats with excited expectation, Erica teasingly asked with a leering grin, "What'a you give me for it?"

"$20 bucks," Bullets answered at once. "We'll each chip in five."

"Yeah," Weasel said seriously, "it'll be the first money you ever make as a professional, and it'll only take a couple of minutes."

"If it takes 10 minutes," Nervous Nate pitched in, quickly calculating, "at $20 dollars, why you'd be makin' a $120 bucks an hour!"

"Not bad pay for an amateur," Fat Bart put in, licking his lips.

"And all the beer you can drink!" Bullets exclaimed, suddenly standing up, taking her hand and guiding her up onto the coffee table.

$20 bucks was a lot of money to the 13-year-old, and not unlike Bullets, she too had reached the pinnacle of her depravity, actually enjoying the hypocrisy her life had become. Egged on by the boys, she began moving to the music.

Twirling about on the coffee table before their excited, upturned faces, she seductively hiked the nightshirt up inch by inch before finally pulling it off and casting it aside. Then the chanting for the panties began.

And with her entire wardrobe of the moment consisting of only two articles of clothing, it wasn't long before, to enthusiastic applause from the audience, she was engaged in her first nude performance - and loving every minute of it, the pink, upturned nipples on her full, gorgeous breasts as firm as her damp, swollen mound.

Their own crotches bulging with the tight, restrictive discomfort of their jeans, as if through some instinctive animal communication the four boys suddenly moved as one. Before Erica knew what was happening, in a drunken swirl of lights and colors, pounding music and motion, they swept her off the table and laid her down on the tiny, carpeted living room floor.

It didn't take her long to figure out what they expected her next performance to involve, and all at once Erica was kicking and screaming furiously. But with Fat Bart on one shoulder, Weasel on the other, and Nervous pegging her legs, it was useless.

"Cover her mouth!" Bullets ordered in a husky voice as he stood over her and unzipped his jeans. As he hiked his pants down and his weapon sprang free fully erect, Erica frantically shook her head with muffled, terror-stricken cries.

"Aw come on, Erica," Bullets grinned, "you're gonna love it! Every girl I've ever been with's loved it. You're just scared 'cause ya never did it before. You just need to be broke is all. Believe me, it's gonna feel sooo good you'll come back beggin' for more! So come on, just lay back and enjoy it. Tomorrow you'll be thankin' me."

"I get seconds!" Weasel called as Bullets shoved his jeans down to his ankles and started to his knees.

*   *   *

"Now you know what to do, right?" Rankin said as he handed Taterhead the little transmitter device. They'd met in the church parking lot. Taterhead would drive his own truck to Weasel's while Rankin parked the squad car a block over to await the signal.

"I know what to do," Taterhead answered evenly, slipping the little transmitter into his pocket. The tiny, electronic microphone was under his shirt, taped to his solar plexus. The wire antenna was wrapped around his body and affixed at the middle of his back.

"Just put this in the bushes by the door as you go up to the house," Rankin instructed, handing him the little tape recorder.

"Right," Taterhead said, taking the small black box.

"And don't forget to turn it on," Rankin said with a smile.

Taterhead nodded.

Looking him over one last time to make sure nothing showed, Rankin said crisply "Okay, let's go."

Taterhead didn't feel nervous at all as he climbed into his old pickup and pulled out of the church parking lot for Weasel's place. After all, he'd gone to many a party at Weasel's over the years. It would be like old times, he kept telling himself. Just going by the Weasel's for a few beers with the old gang. That's all.

Since the driveway was full with everybody's cars, he parked on the street out front, got out, walked up to the little porch, paused to switch on the recorder, stuck it in the bushes, and then hesitated at the bottom of the steps.

From inside he could hear the thump of music, the loud voices and the laughter. In the old days he would have just walked right in as everybody did. Well, this wasn't the old days, he reasoned, but it was *like* the old days. As he and Rankin had discussed, if he walked right in like he belonged there, for a moment it would feel that way to them, too - and that was the psychological factor that would give them pause long enough for him to get the little charade started.

Taking a deep breath, he mounted the steps, twisted the knob and pushed the door open to be greeted by an orgiastic scene straight out of Dante's vision of hell.

*   *   *

Stretched out in his favorite chair in front of the TV with a cold one, his wife Eva Marie next to him reading, Axl Erickson picked up the phone on the first ring. Kevin Crisper had decided to hell with it, he was getting out and had called Erica to arrange a little midnight rendezvous. It was 11:15 PM.

"Well, I'll see," Axl said into the phone, "but Erica said she was going to bed. Just a minute." He set the phone down and turned to his wife. "Honey, you wanna see if Erica's asleep yet?"

With a sigh she set her book face-down to hold her place, got up, and went down the hall to her daughter's bedroom only to return a moment later looking bewildered. "Erica's not here," she said.

Looking surprised, Axl picked up the receiver, said simply, "She's sleeping Kevin, I'll tell her you called," and hung up.

"Damn that girl!" he said, heaving himself out of his chair.

"Where're you going?" his wife asked with concern.

"To find Erica," he said, "and kick her ass all the way back home. And I've got a pretty good idea where that ass is, too."

"Where?"

He paused at the door and turned. "Where else? Probably at Weasel's. He has a party every Friday night." And then he was gone.

Storming past Rankin sitting in his police cruiser at the end of the block, Axl didn't pay him any mind. With all that had happened in the last few months they weren't exactly on the best of terms, and the last thing he wanted to admit to Rankin was that his daughter was sneaking out at night to be with the town's bad boy party crowd.

Seeing Axl stride by with rapid determination in the direction of Weasel's, Rankin thought, *good, maybe the bastard's going over to the party and we'll nail him in the sting too!*

*   *   *

For one interminable moment Taterhead stood in the doorway frozen to inaction, stunned to disbelief at the sight of a naked Erica spread-eagled on the floor on her back and held down by Fat Bart, Weasel, and Nervous, with Bullets, his jeans and underwear down around his ankles, about to mount the weeping, struggling child.

Caught, literally, with his pants down and feeling very foolish, Bullets twisted around to see what everyone else was gaping at and couldn't believe his eyes. . . .

All at once infuriated and sickened at the sight of four grown men caught in the act of brutally raping a child as if they were a pack of wild dogs, in a white-hot rage Taterhead grabbed the heavy steel floor lamp and swung with all his might. The heavy circular steel base thunked off Nervous Nate's head with a sickening thud, knocking him out cold and leaving him sprawled across Bullets, who was now on the floor on his side pinned beneath the boy's deadweight. With his jeans threatening to come completely off every time he tried to drag himself out from under Nervous, Bullets struggled frantically to pull them up.

But that wasn't Taterhead's concern. Letting the momentum of the heavy lamp carry him around, he speared it right at Fat Bart just as the big drunk hunkered down and threw the full bulk of his weight into rushing him like a linebacker - headlong into the solid steel base. It reverberated with a ringing *bong!* that sent the big boy staggering backwards where he fell in a tangled heap to the floor.

Moments later, dazed and confused, his right arm twisted behind his back and pinned by the weight of his own body, he was amazed and horrified to discover he couldn't move. Suffering from a spinal neck injury that would leave him a quadriplegic for the rest of his life, he couldn't even roll off his own arm.

With Erica shrieking hysterically and frantically climbing naked through the rubble of the broken up living room trying to find her clothes, and Weasel long gone out the back door, Taterhead turned to Bullets. Breathing heavily, he stood over him with the lamp raised high while Bullets, finally freed of Nervous, lay on his back on the floor pulling up his jeans.

"Make one move to get up off that floor and you're dead!" Taterhead said tightly.

With the withered, whimpering cries for help from Fat Bart in his ears, and scared to death, Bullets remained on the floor, his eyes huge and pleading as he begged, "Please don't hit me, Tater, please, I won't move."

With his back to the door and his eyes on Bullets, Taterhead rested the floor lamp on one shoulder and was reaching for the transmitter in his pocket when a stunned Axl Erickson filled the doorway.

Taking one look at his naked, hysterical daughter frantically pulling on her panties, he growled like a grizzly bear, leaped across the room, slammed Taterhead to the wall as the lamp crashed to the floor, and held him pinned by the throat. "I'm gonna kill ya, you little bastard!" he snarled maniacally and unsheathed the big buck knife.

But before he could make another move his daughter was all over him, kicking and flailing away at his back and crying with earsplitting shrieks, "Leave him alone! It was Bullets! Bullets did everything!" And then she collapsed at his feet, clinging to his legs as she confessed through hysterical sobs of the most bitter remorse the lie about the eggs, Tater trying to lure them to the woods - everything.

Looking at Taterhead, then his daughter, then back at Taterhead, the big man suddenly dropped his knife and burst into tears. Releasing the boy, he sank to his knees and embraced his wailing daughter.

With her face buried in his shoulder and her crying reduced to muffled sobbing, Axl raised teary eyes to Taterhead, his voice quavering as he begged, "Please. . . please forgive me."

Trembling with every emotion from anger to fear to sorrow for the poor, wretched people around him, Taterhead heaved a tired sigh and slowly nodded. "I'll certainly try, Mr. Erickson," he said softly, "as best I can."

And with that he slipped around the heap of human tragedy at his feet, dug the transmitter from his pocket and held it out in the palm of his hand. The plastic casing was broken in two, mangled wires hanging out.

And then he noticed Bullets was gone.

OTHER DREAMS

THIRTY-SEVEN

OTHER DREAMS REALIZED

With Erica's confession widely circulated, a process started by her own father, Kevin Crisper and Johnny Bulger both came forward as well.   Under close questioning they even admitted their sexual encounter with Bullets and acknowledged that they'd felt compelled to service him out of fear that he would have told on them if they hadn't.

To make matters worse for Bullets, with Weasel facing the same attempted sexual assault charges, he admitted it was Bullets driving the "mystery car", and related how Bullets had initiated the accident.   He also admitted, along with Nervous Nate and a bedside confession from Fat Bart, both of whom were also thusly charged, that in fact they had never actually caught Taterhead Ellis and Gaitlin Tyler in a homosexual liaison.

Now that the whole truth of the matter was out a lot of lives were forever changed.   Some for the better, some for the worse.   By far Bartholomew "Fat Bart" Binks fared the worst, forever bound to a bed or strapped into a wheelchair, unable even to feed himself or scratch an itch on his nose.

Furthermore, there was no insurance and no one to sue. Taterhead was absolved of any responsibility for Bart's injuries on grounds that it was, number one, self-defense, and number two, certainly not intentional.   In fact, Fat Bart was as much to blame as anyone for having drunkenly run headlong into the lamp base in the first place. Thus with no financial support, Fat Bart would not be long for professional nursing care. And then his poor mother would have to change his diapers daily.

Nathaniel   "Nervous Nate"   Naumann suffered a concussion in the melee, but after a three day stay in the hospital, was fully recovered.

Axl stopped going to church and started praying. For a good heart. For a good soul. For to become a patient man slow to anger. He stopped going around with a big buck knife strapped to his waist and became a rather quiet, soft-spoken man. He felt he'd escaped a close brush with hell - and was sure he saw it in Bullets' eyes every time he looked at the boy throughout his trial.

Pastor Robert Renfrow, considered by the community an utter failure as a spiritual leader, had become something of a social pariah. When church attendance dropped to nearly zero he was transferred to another city in another state, replaced by a grave, elderly gentleman named Stephen Peterson.

Jim and Anna O'Brien, torn by the loss of their daughter and disgraced by their son, divorced, sold off their holdings and moved away. In the shuffle, Taterhead, with the help of a bank loan, managed to buy back the 40 acres the O'Brien's had purchased from old man Ellis a little over a year ago.

In November, just before Thanksgiving, two corrupt Jefferson County sheriff's deputies, Bill   "Barnacle Bill" Barnickle and his partner, Ted   "Dashing Ted"   Dasher, were suspended with pay until an investigation was resolved of an incident in which they nearly stomped a Latino youth to death. According to the officers the youth had become violent in resisting arrest. Unfortunately (for the youth) Barnacle Bill and Dashing Ted had been out of reefer for a week and had been unusually irritable. But not to worry. With the paid vacation the stomping had earned them, they were going to make a quick trip out to the coast for a little **R&R** and a Kilo of fine California Red Bud a friend raised hydroponically in his basement.

Kelsy "Bullets" O'Brien, Henry "The Weasel" Hillard, Nathaniel "Nervous Nate" Naumann, and Bartholomew "Fat Bart" Binks were all charged with attempted criminal sexual assault. In addition, Bullets, for his sexual encounter with Kevin Crisper and Johnny Bulger, was also charged with aggravated criminal sexual abuse of a minor. Under the Illinois penal code, attempted criminal sexual assault is a class-one felony punishable by not less than four, nor more than 15 years in prison. In addition, a fine of up to 10 thousand dollars may also be imposed.

For his part, Bullets was sentenced to 10 years for the attempted sexual assault and four years on the sexual abuse charge. The other three boys were sentenced to seven years respectively, with Bart's sentence suspended due to his medical condition.

When Gaitlin had returned to the court house exactly one month after his first hearing, this time there had been no protesters. Due to the mitigating circumstances in Gaitlin's case, aided of course by the evidence Rankin produced, including Weasel's confession and Rory Calhoun's testimony, the state dropped the charge of reckless homicide. On the first-offense DUI charge the judge imposed a sentence of time served plus six months probation. Fully recovered from the injuries received in the Gray Wolf Tap brawl, Gaitlin walked out a free man, his conscience at ease. He would be returning to work in the spring when construction crews started up again.

It was mid-December now and flurries were just starting to fall as Taterhead, Blackjack beside him, pulled into the Tyler's gas station. With all that had happened in the last four months, a remorseful and apologetic community went out of their way to buy fuel or have their vehicles serviced at the Tyler station. Thus with business booming, George and Marybell Tyler had taken their house off the market. And now, with Sammy busy on a brake job, George came out of the garage wiping his hands on a rag.

"Hi, Mr. Tyler," Taterhead said as he and Blackjack climbed out of the truck for a stretch.

"Hey Tater, Blackjack," George returned the greeting with a nod. "Say, I see you got the gates back up on your pickup. Gonna buy another cow?" he grinned.

"Nah," Tater shook his head, "I'm gonna pick up a goat I bought."

"A goat!" George exclaimed.

"Yeah, I'm gonna learn to make goat cheese, too."

With a half-shake of his head, George said, "I tell ya, you're an ambitious young man." He paused, "What can I do for you?"

"Fill 'er up, Mr. Tyler."

"Yes sir!" George Tyler smiled big and turned to the gas pumps.

After he and Blackjack got the goat loaded, home, and unloaded, they were going to get the plow mounted. Every business and home owner that didn't plow their own driveways or shovel their own walks had contracted the work out to Taterhead. It was almost more work than he could handle, but with Blackjack's help he was sure he could get it done - and they'd both make a decent wage.

The snow was falling hard and fast now and starting to stick. Turning to Blackjack, Taterhead said, "See if you can catch a snowflake on your tongue," and then with a grinning Blackjack looking on, he turned his face up to the sky and tried.

It was going to be a good year, too. A *very* good year. Taterhead could just tell.

※   ※   ※